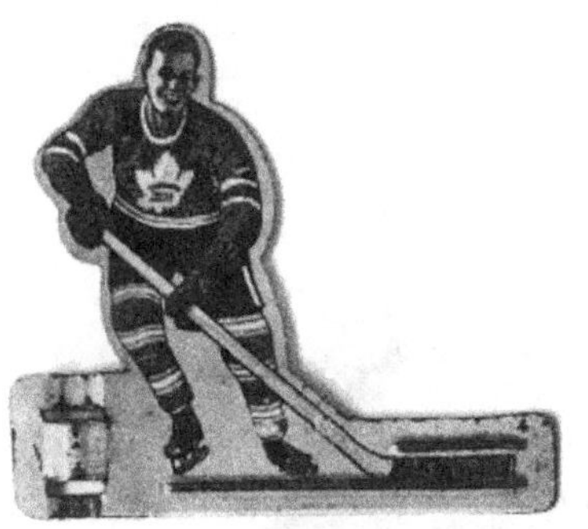

Treyf Books

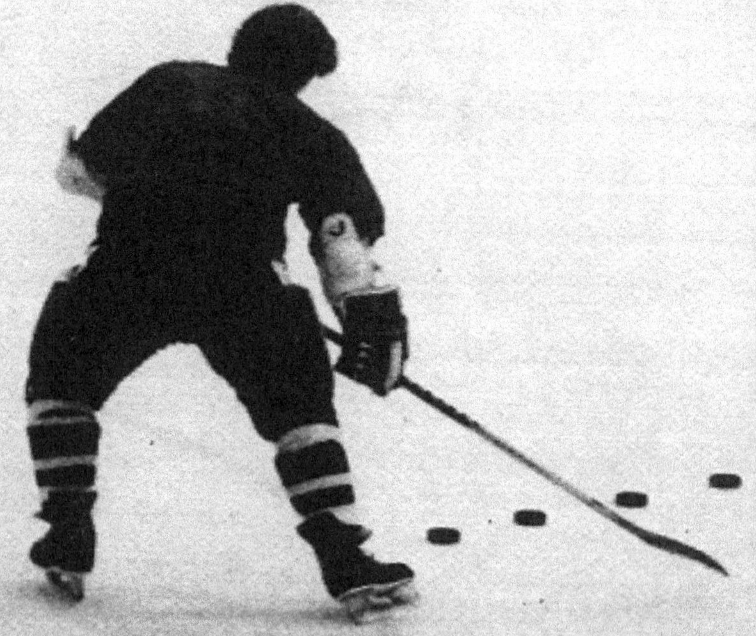

Games Oligopolists Play

by Rob Kovitz

Treyf 25th Anniversary edition 2013

Published by Treyf Books
5-193 Furby Street
Winnipeg, MB Canada R3C 2A6
www.treyf.com
keeprefrigerated@treyf.com

LIBRARY AND ARCHIVES CANADA CATALOGUING IN PUBLICATION

Kovitz, Rob, 1963–, author, artist
Games oligopolists play / by Rob Kovitz.—Treyf 25th anniversary edition.

Includes bibliographical reference.
Issued in print and electronic formats.
ISBN 978-0-9812869-7-6 (pbk.).—ISBN 978-0-9812869-8-3 (epub)

1. Kovitz, Rob, 1963-. 2. Artists' books--Canada. I. Title.

N7433.4.K68G68 2013 700.971 C2013-905711-0
C2013-905712-9

Financial assistance for the creation and production of Treyf Books is sometimes provided by the Canada Council for the Arts, the Manitoba Arts Council, and the City of Winnipeg through the Winnipeg Arts Council.

Canada Council for the Arts Conseil des arts du Canada

MANITOBA ARTS COUNCIL
CONSEIL DES ARTS DU MANITOBA

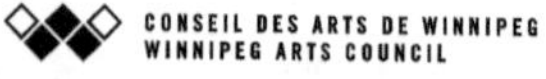

Dedicated to all the goalies.

10 9 8 7 6 5 4 3 2 1

PLAYER'S CONTRACT

AS PRESCRIBED FOR THE

National Hockey League

The ....

Of .... WITH Joe Hall

I hereby certify that I have, at this date, received, examined and noted of record the within Contract, and that it is in regular form.

.... President National Hockey League.

Regular Contract:— ....

Approved 191

☞ IMPORTANT NOTICE TO PLAYERS AND CLUB PRESIDENTS ☜

Every player before signing a contract should carefully scrutinize the same to ascertain whether all of the conditions agreed upon between the Player and Club President have been incorporated therein, and if any have been omitted the player should insist upon having all the terms, conditions, promises and agreements inserted in the contract before he signs the same.

NATIONAL HOCKEY LEAGUE

PLAYER'S CONTRACT (REGULAR)

Articles of Agreement between the Canadian Hockey Club Inc.

of the City Montreal, in the Province of Quebec

a club member of a League known as the "National Hockey League", party of the first part, hereinafter called the Club

and Joe Hall of the City of Brandon in the Province of Manitoba, party of the second part, hereinafter called the Player.

Witnesseth:

That in consideration of the mutual obligations herein and hereby assumed, the parties to this contract severally agree as follows:

1. The club agrees to pay the player for the season of 1918-9, beginning on or about the 10th day of December, 1918, and ending on or about the 25th day of March, 1919, a salary at the rate of $600.00 Six hundred dollars for such season; and an additional sum at the rate of $100.00 One hundred dollars for such season, said additional sum being in consideration of the option herein reserved to the club in Clause 10 hereof; said additional sum to be paid whether said option is exercised or not, making the total compensation to the player for the season herein contracted for $700.00 Seven hundred dollars, and a bonus of one hundred dollars if the club finish in first place and fifty dollars only if the club finish in second place.

Preface

In writing this volume I intend to employ questionable premises and use them to obtain questionable conclusions.

This may seem a goal of doubtful merit, but it is superior to its alternative.

William J. Baumol, Business Behavior and Growth

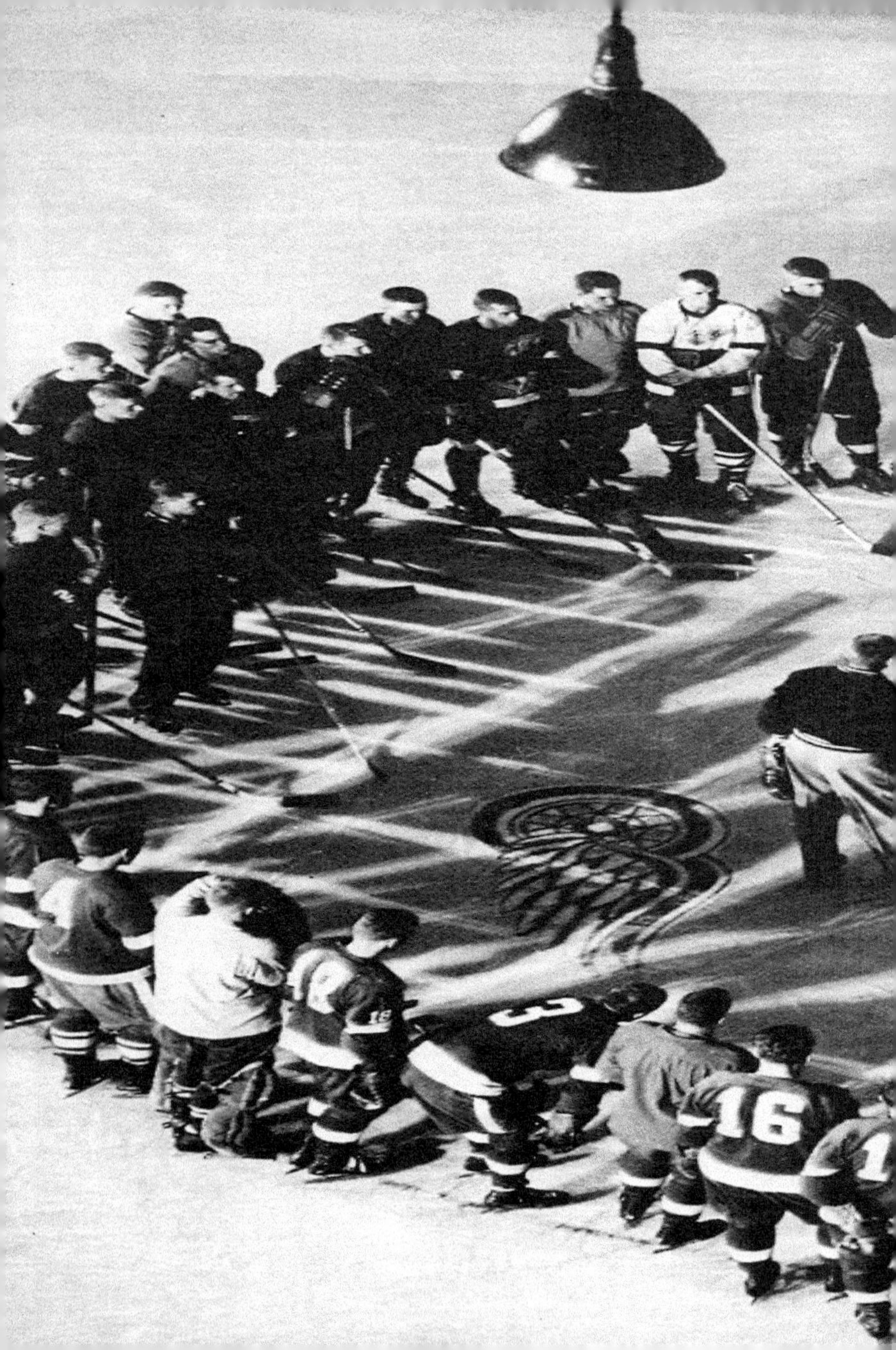

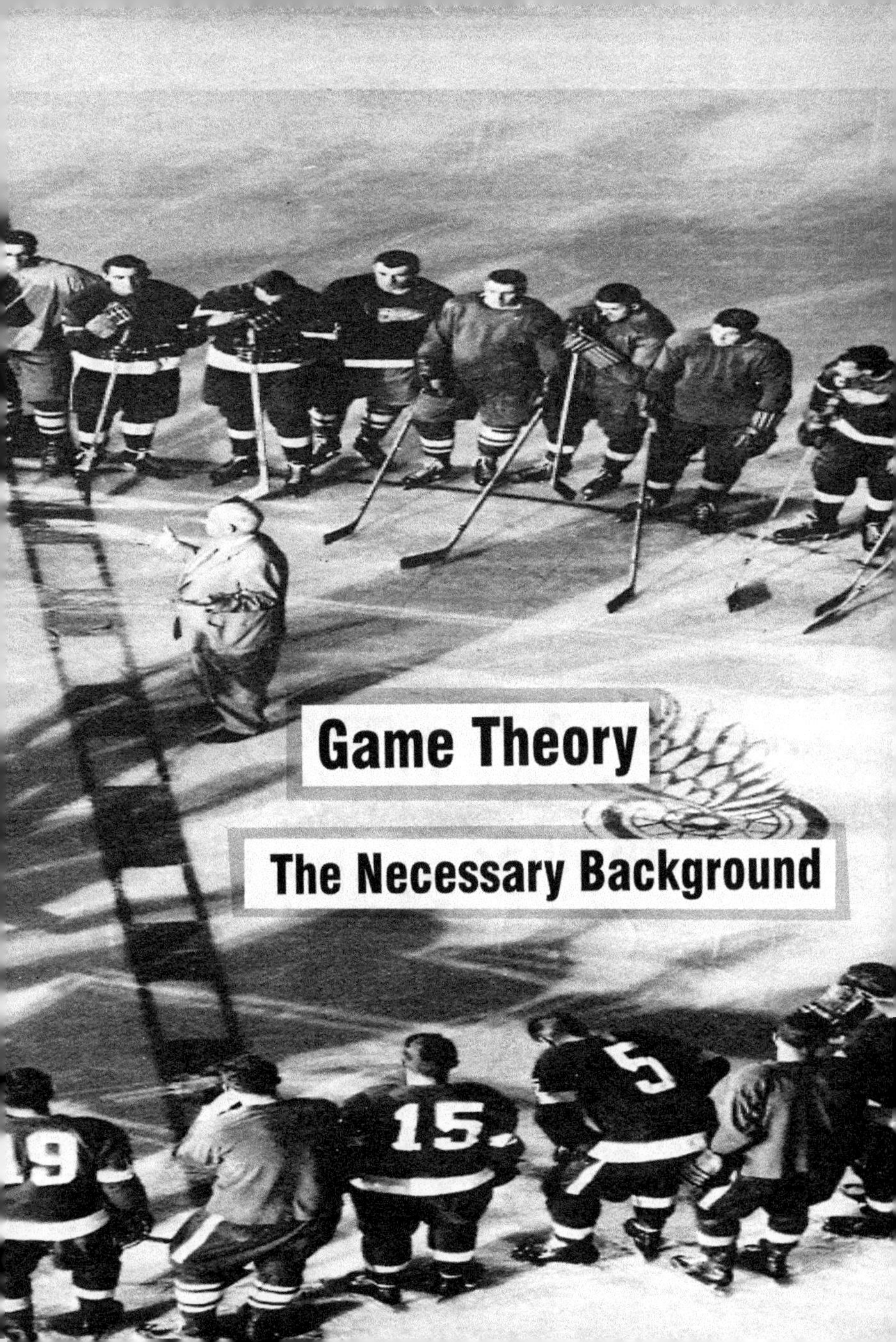
Game Theory
The Necessary Background
19
15
5

Oligopoly—like international diplomacy, labor-management negotiations, and so on—is one of the speediest and most thrilling of sports.

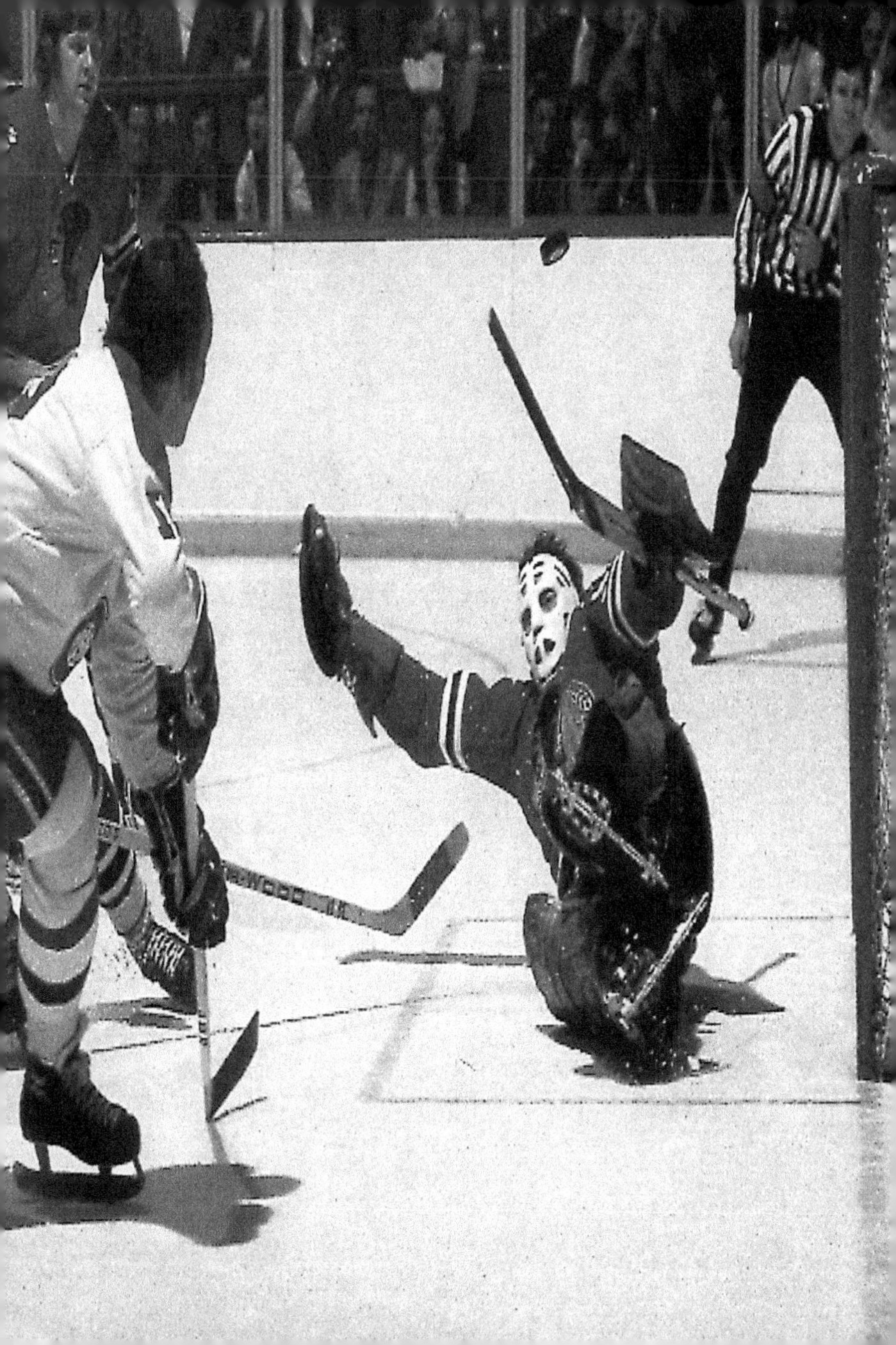

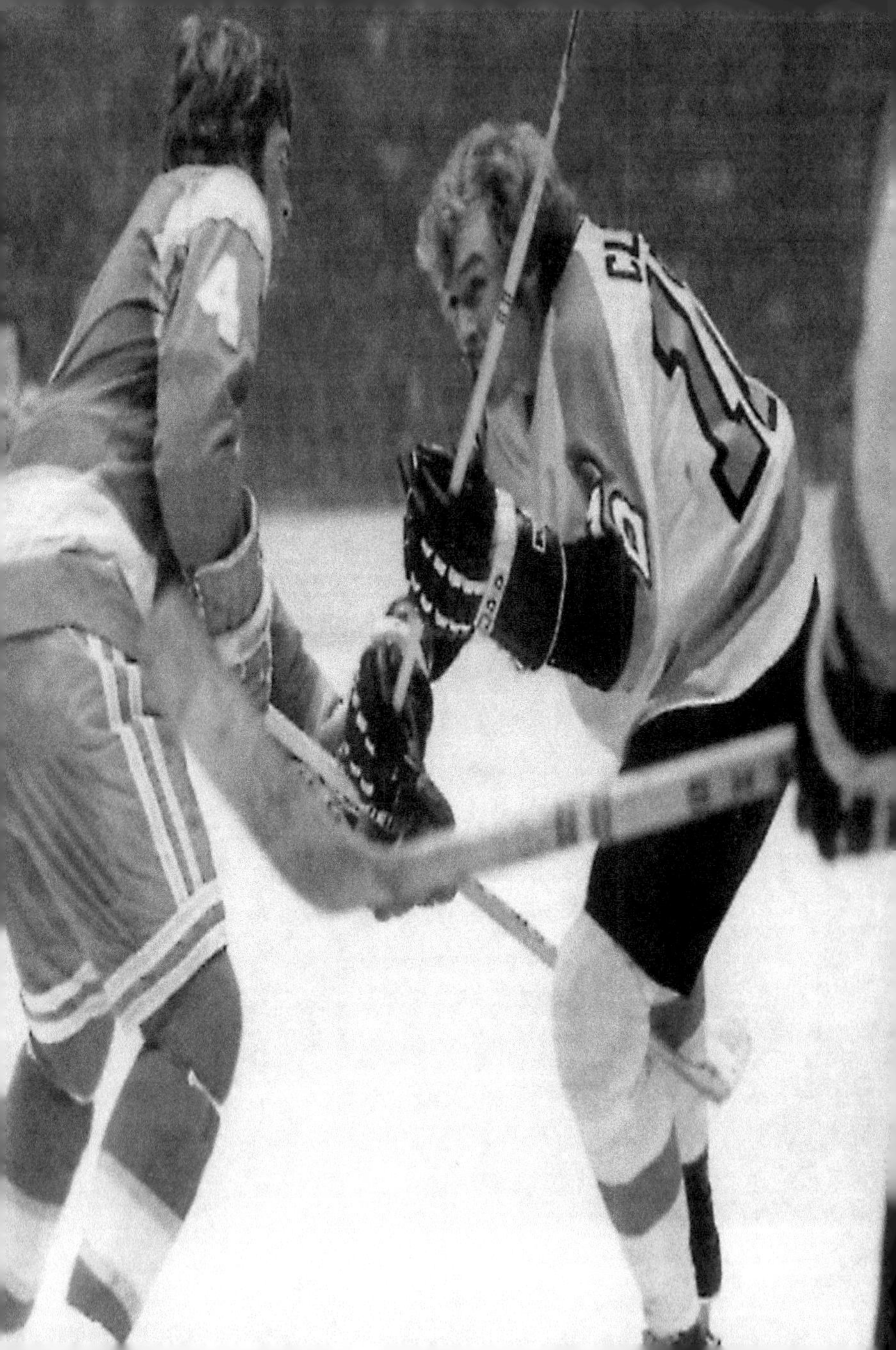

All players wear long and thick gloves.

The crucial feature of any game is that each participant bases his decisions on what he expects the others to do, and therefore on what he thinks the others expect him to do, and indeed on what he thinks the others think he expects them to do, and so on.

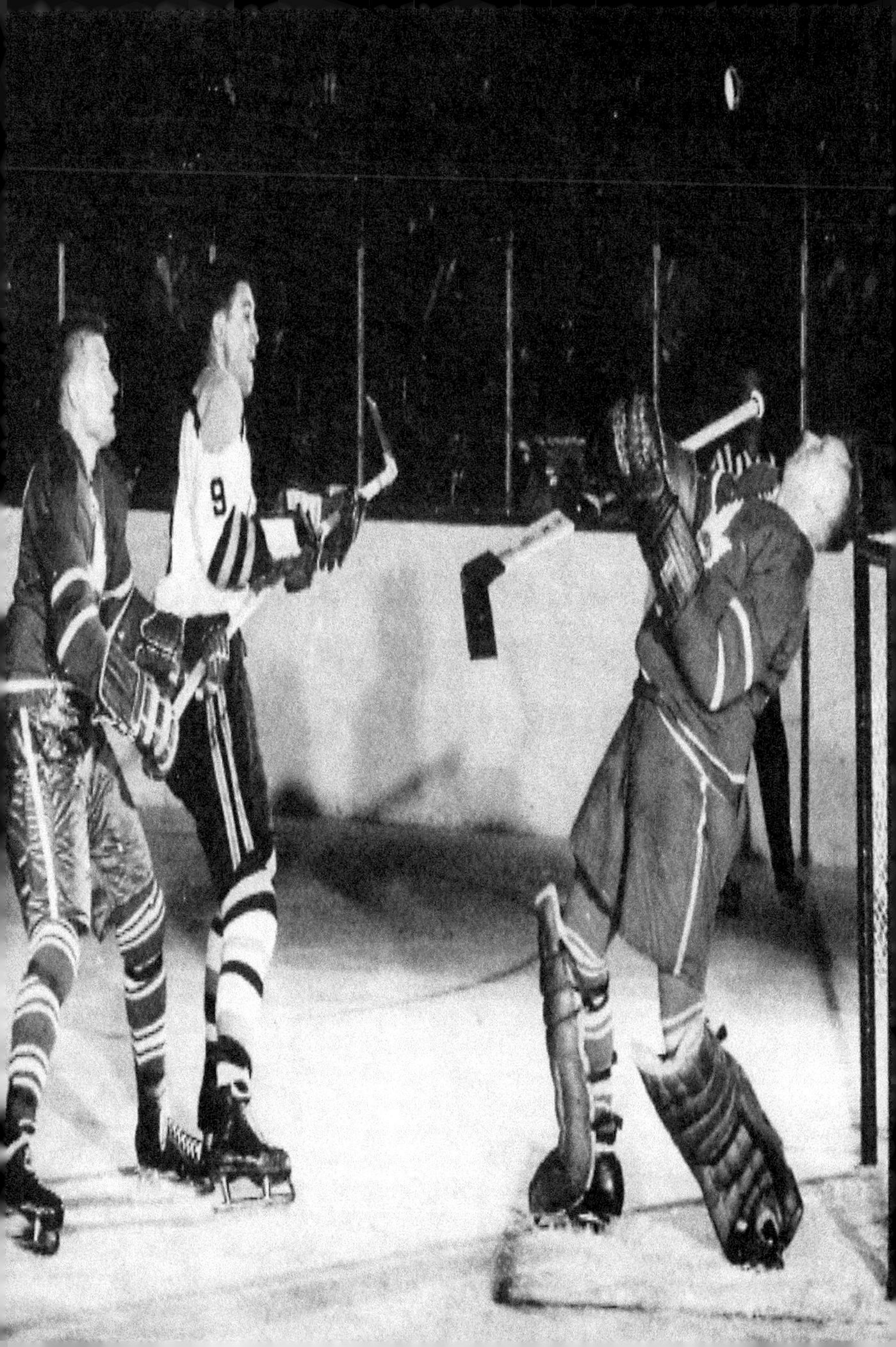
9

"We just didn't compete for pucks the way we usually compete for pucks."

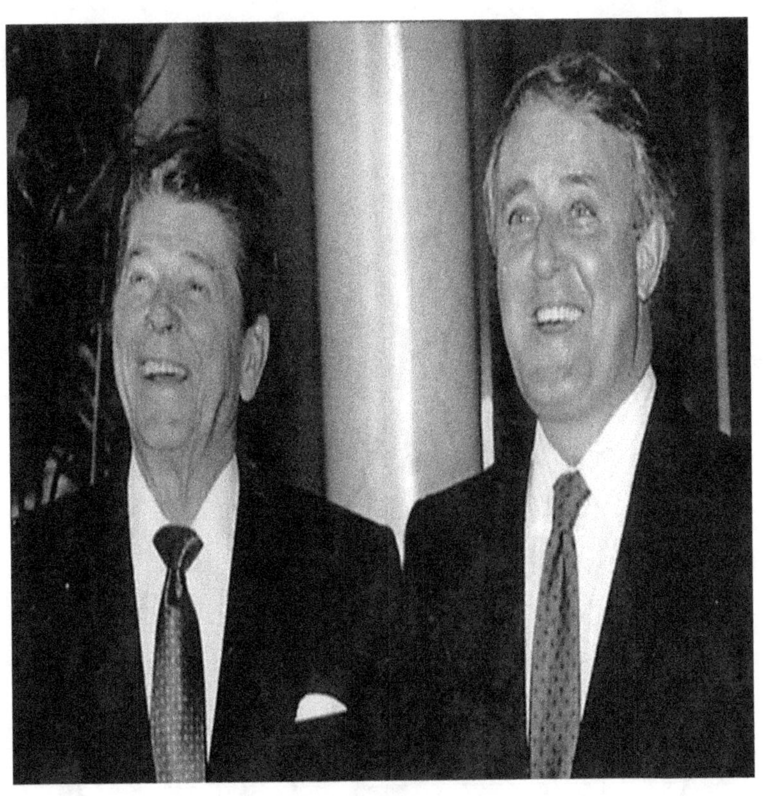

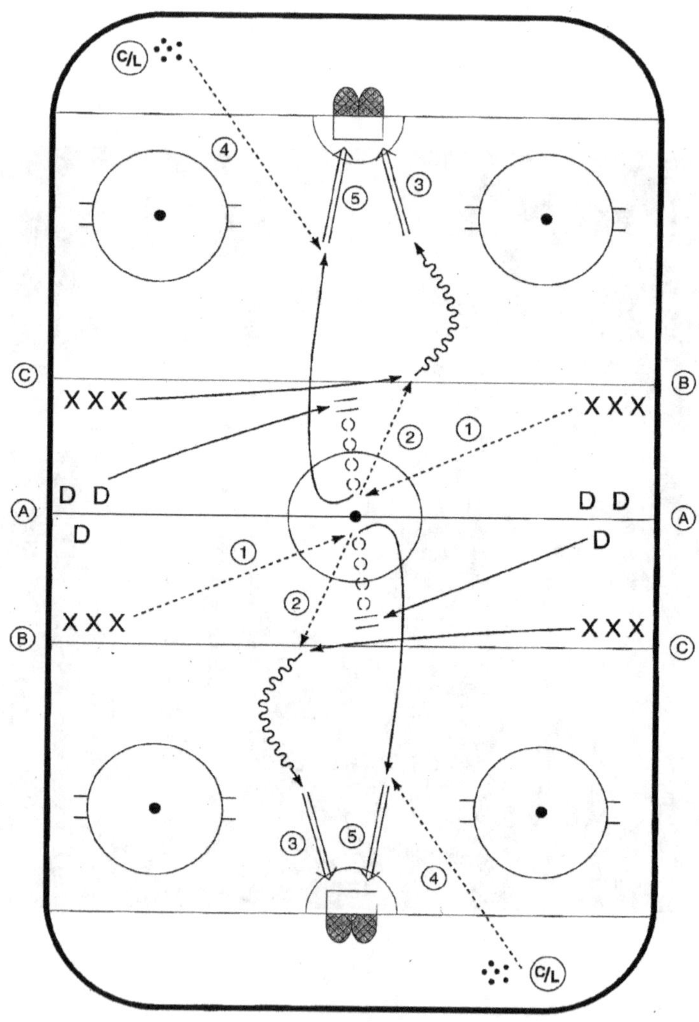

Speed Drill: The Neutral Zone Bump

The term *play* describes a set of moves used by all the players from the start to the end of a game. A description of the way in which two teams carry out negotiations, fix production rates, divide a market, and work out a joint pricing policy illustrates a *play*.

Avoiding risk is the most important skill. A player must be able to turn sharply, skate backwards, and perform many other maneuvers—all at top speed. His subterfuges must be so skillful that he can make any maneuver without taking attention from the game.

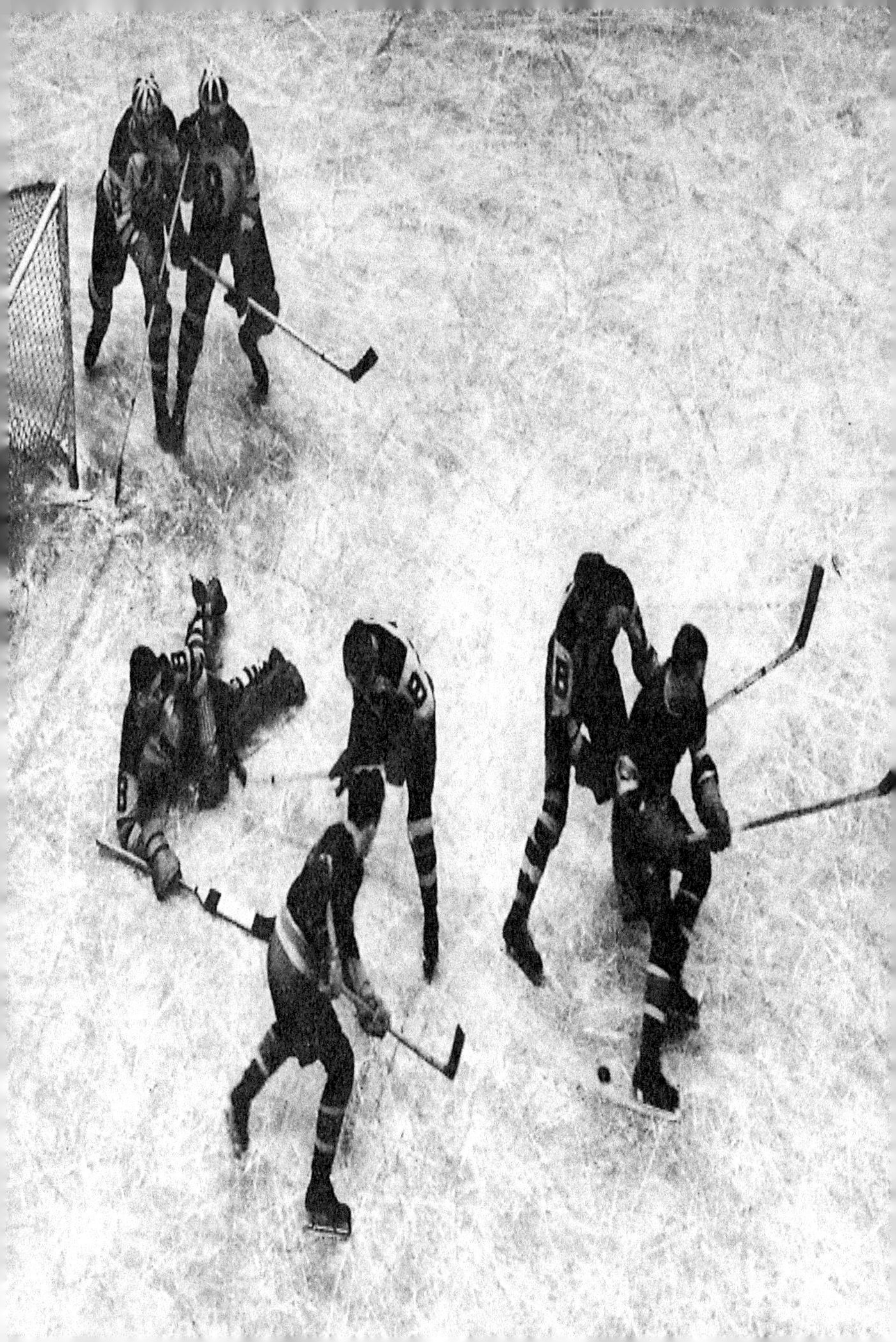

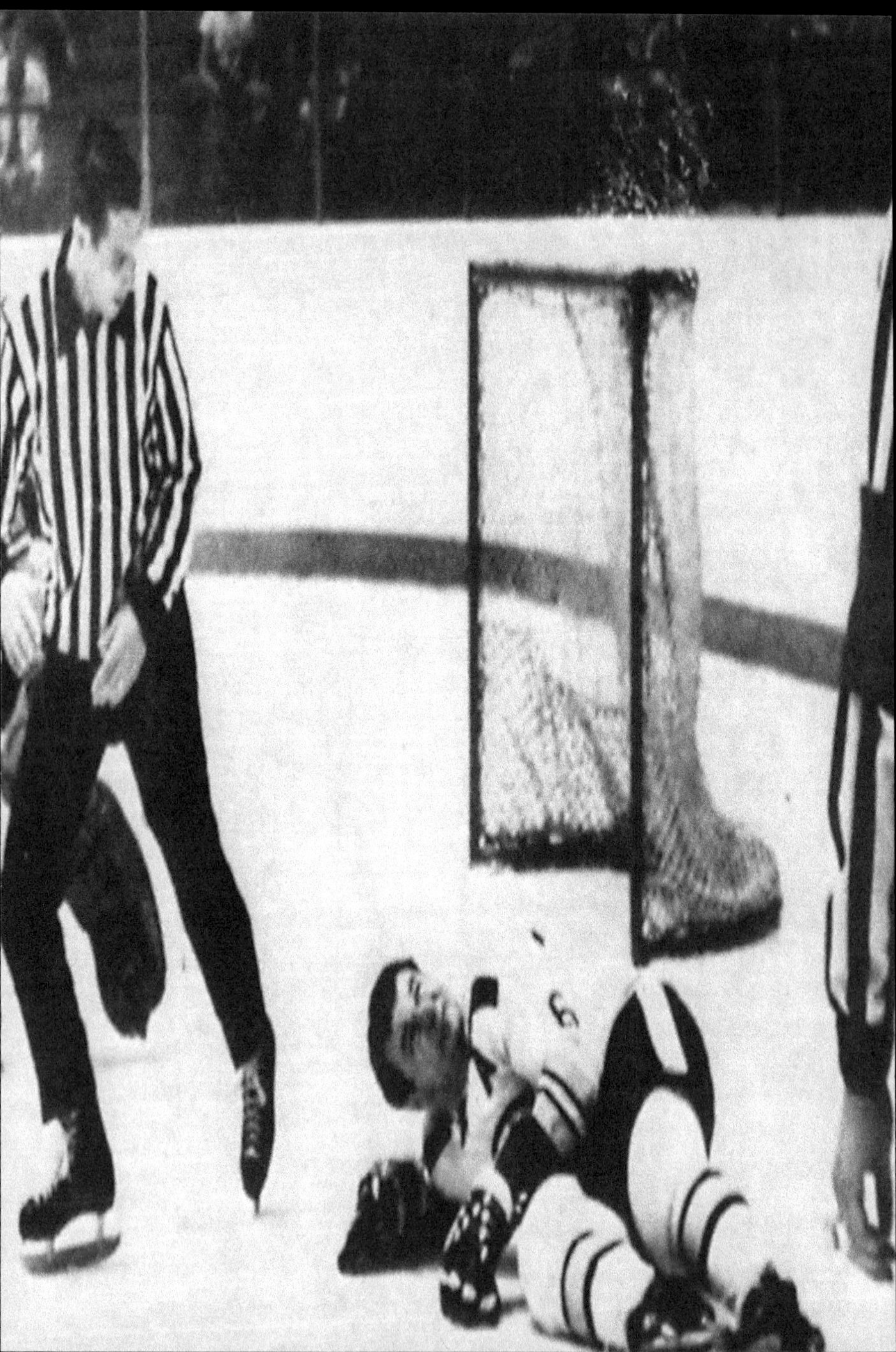

Players are allowed to kick the puck. But a goal can not be scored by kicking a puck into it unless the puck first hits a defending player.

A number of penalties are provided for violating the rules of the game. There are five kinds of penalties in all: 1) minor penalties; 2) major penalties; 3) match penalties; 4) misconduct penalties; 5) minor and major penalty shots.

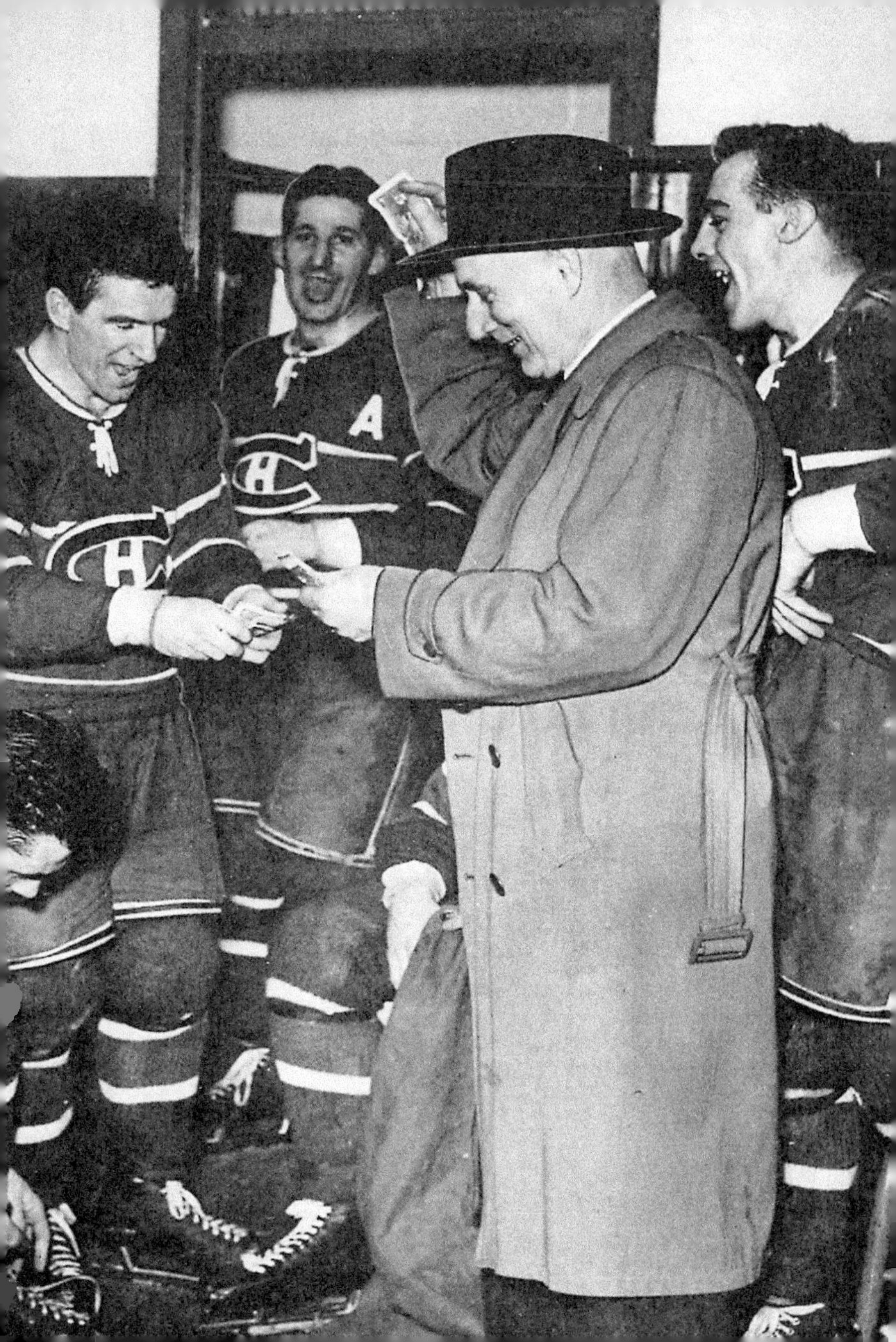

Teams differ in the extent to which they can be differentiated.

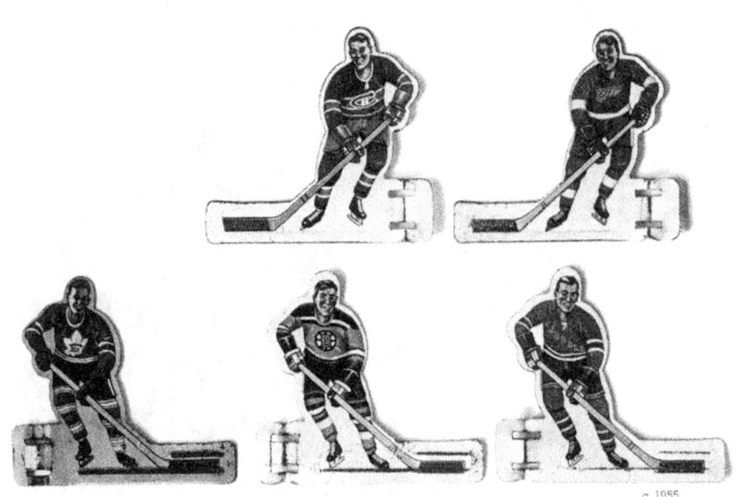

c. 1955

Strategy

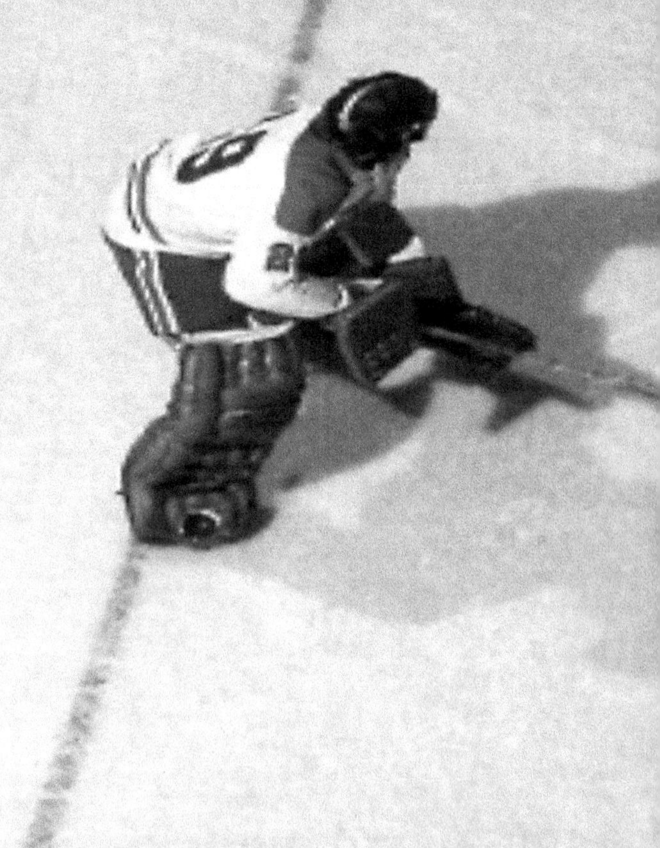

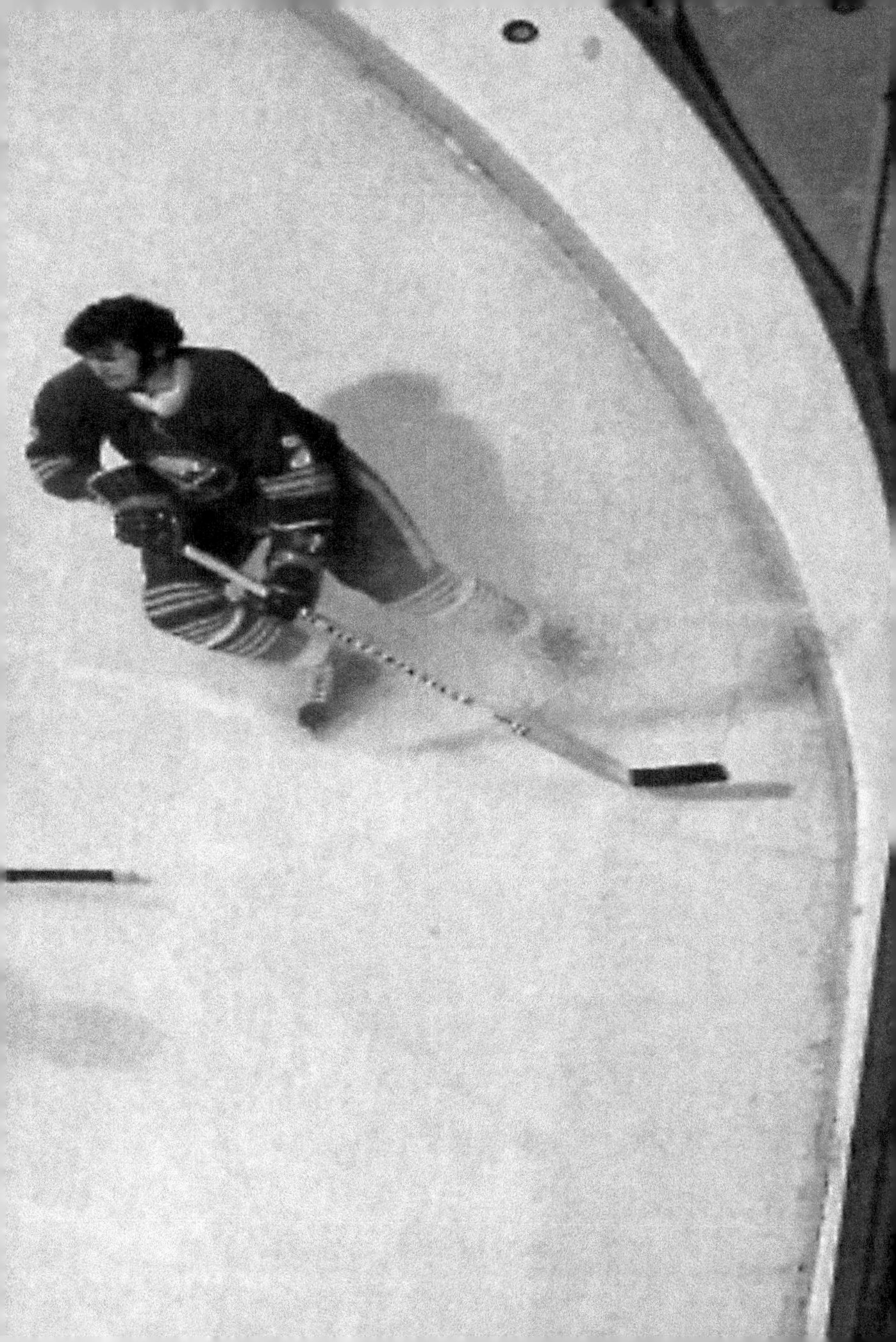

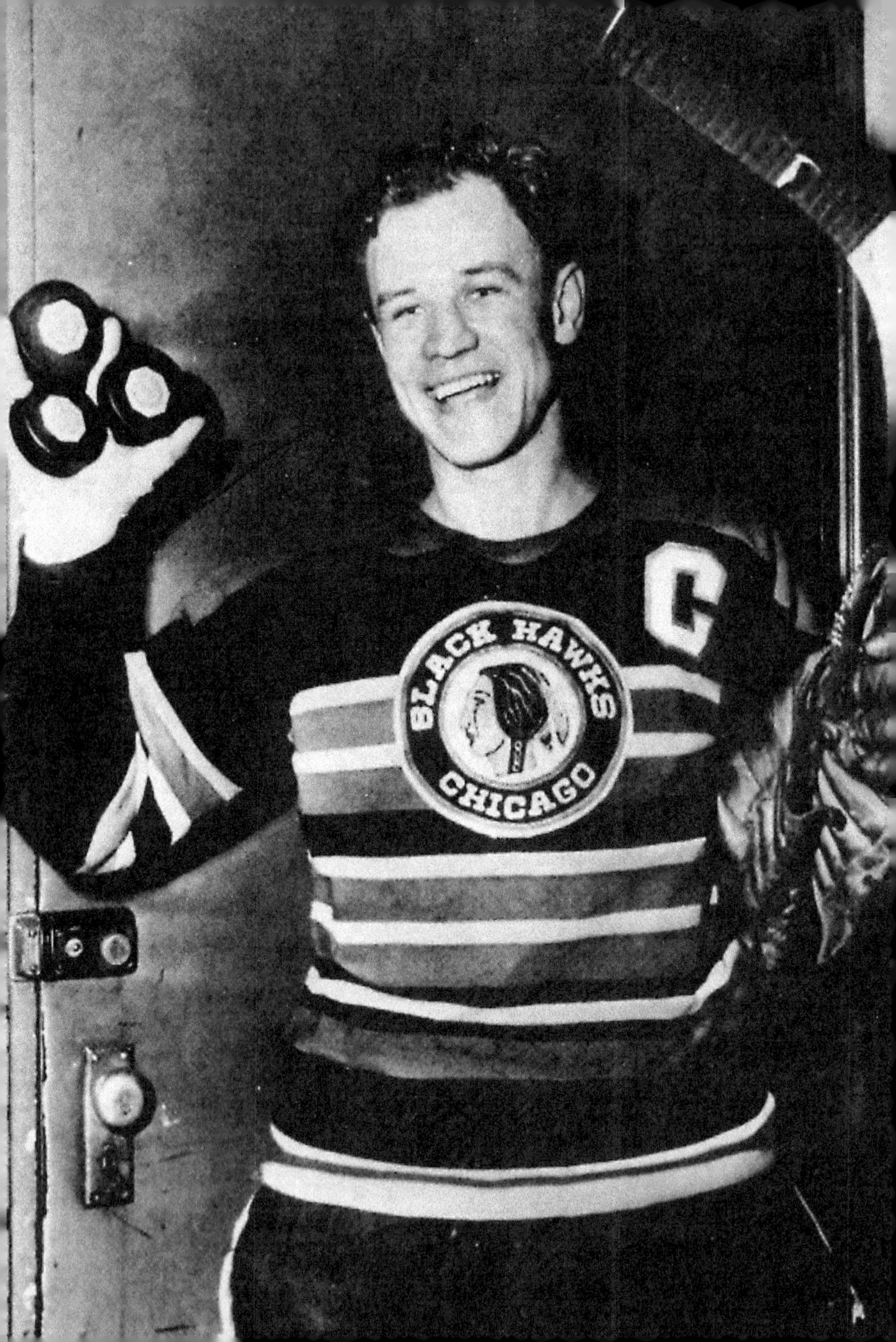
C
BLACK HAWKS
CHICAGO

The notion of a strategy can be made clear by means of a simple example. Consider a game in which each player has only one move. At his turn each player has to choose one of the numbers, 1 or 2. If both players pick the same number, then the first player wins a dollar and the second loses a dollar. If they pick different numbers, then the first loses a dollar and the second wins the same amount.

Suppose, though, that we make this a decidedly "unfair" game, in the sense that we force the first player to move first and allow the second player to be informed of the move chosen by his opponent. It is obvious that the second player will always be able to win.

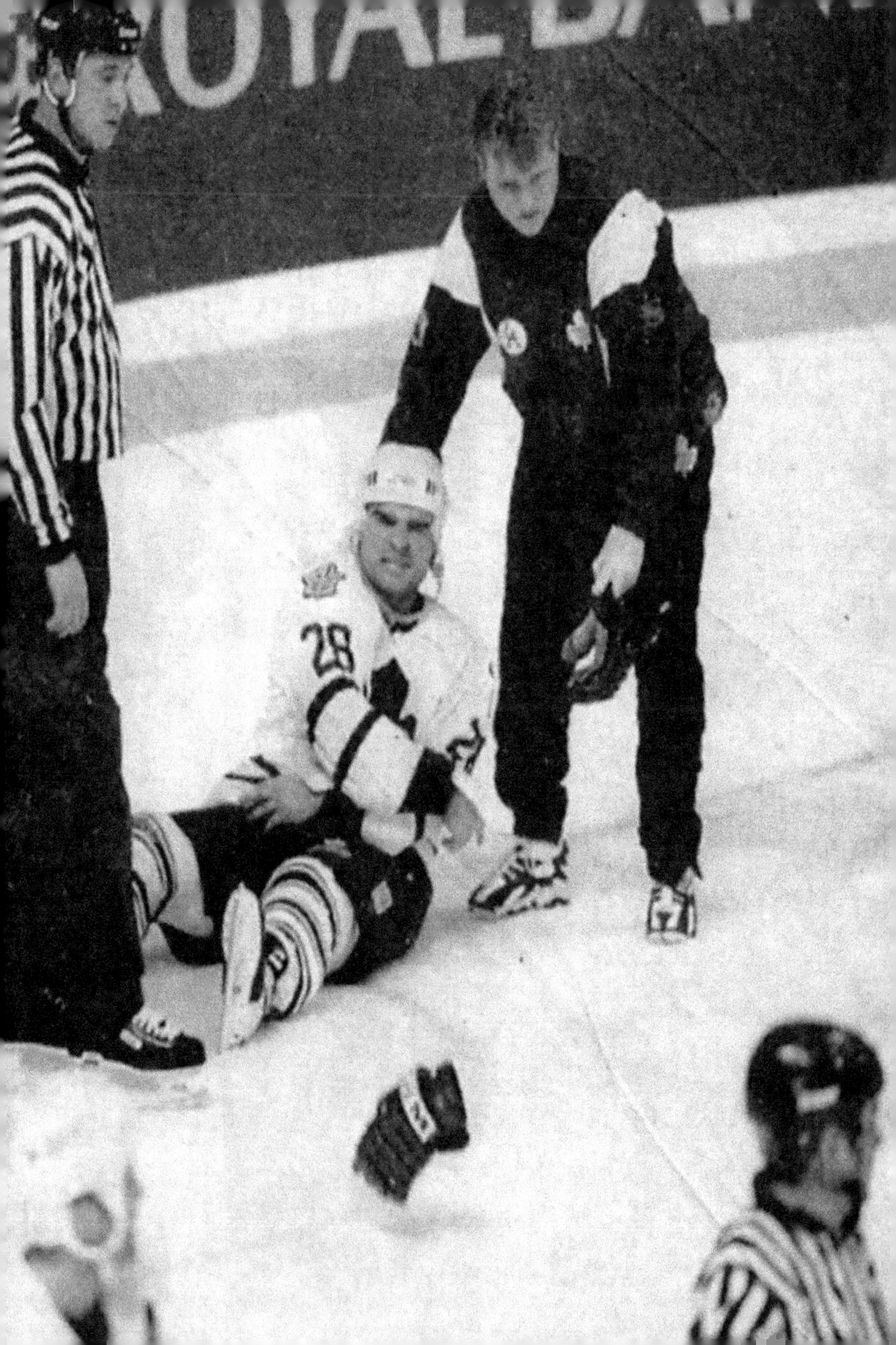
ROYAL
28

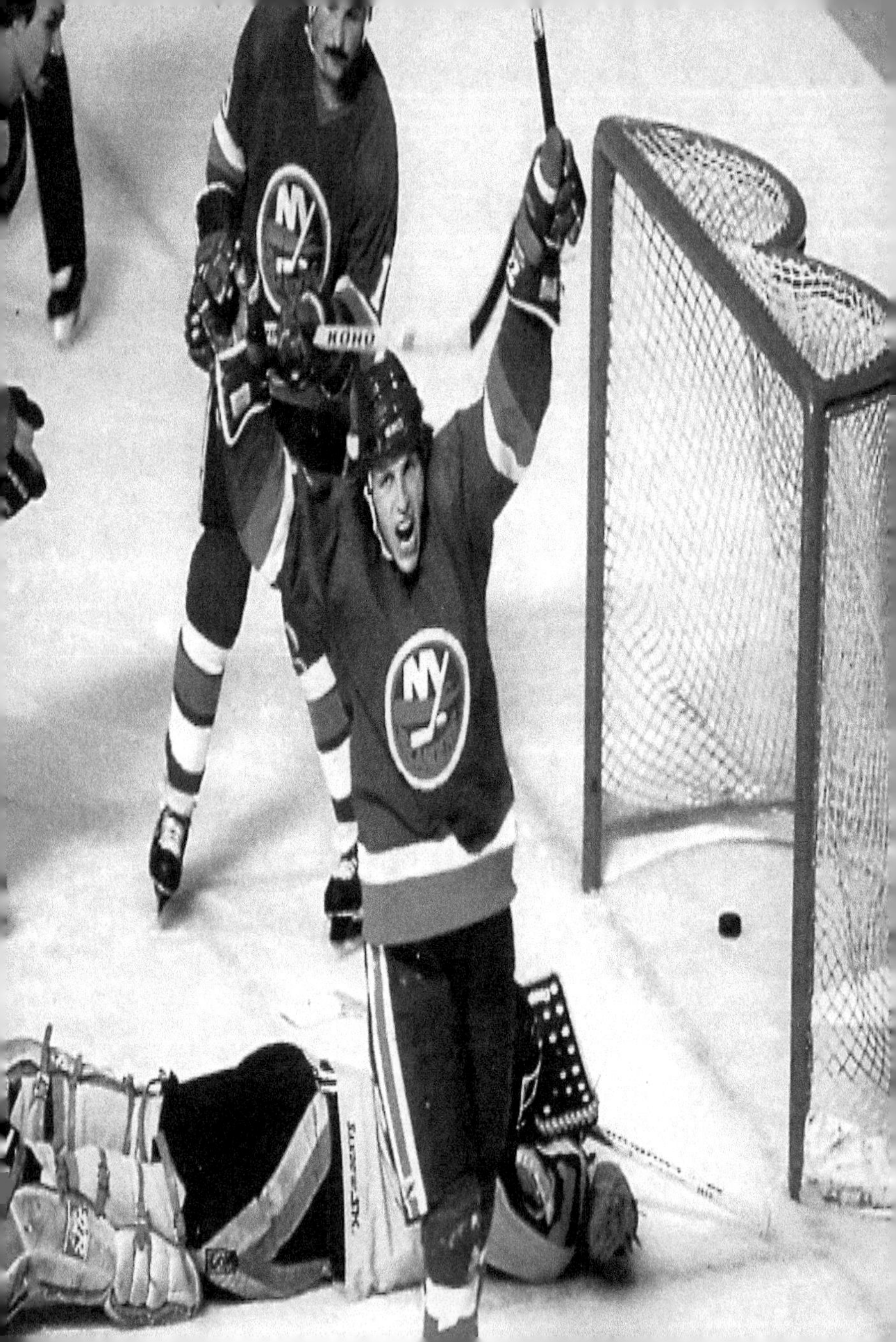
NY
KOHO
NY

Now suppose that the second player could not be bothered to wait around until the first had moved. He could submit to the referee a document which would state: if he chooses 1, I choose 2; if he chooses 2, I choose 1.

**Sound simple?
You bet it is.**

"One of the key elements to winning a face-off is cheating. You've got to cheat because it's too difficult to win most of them fair and square."

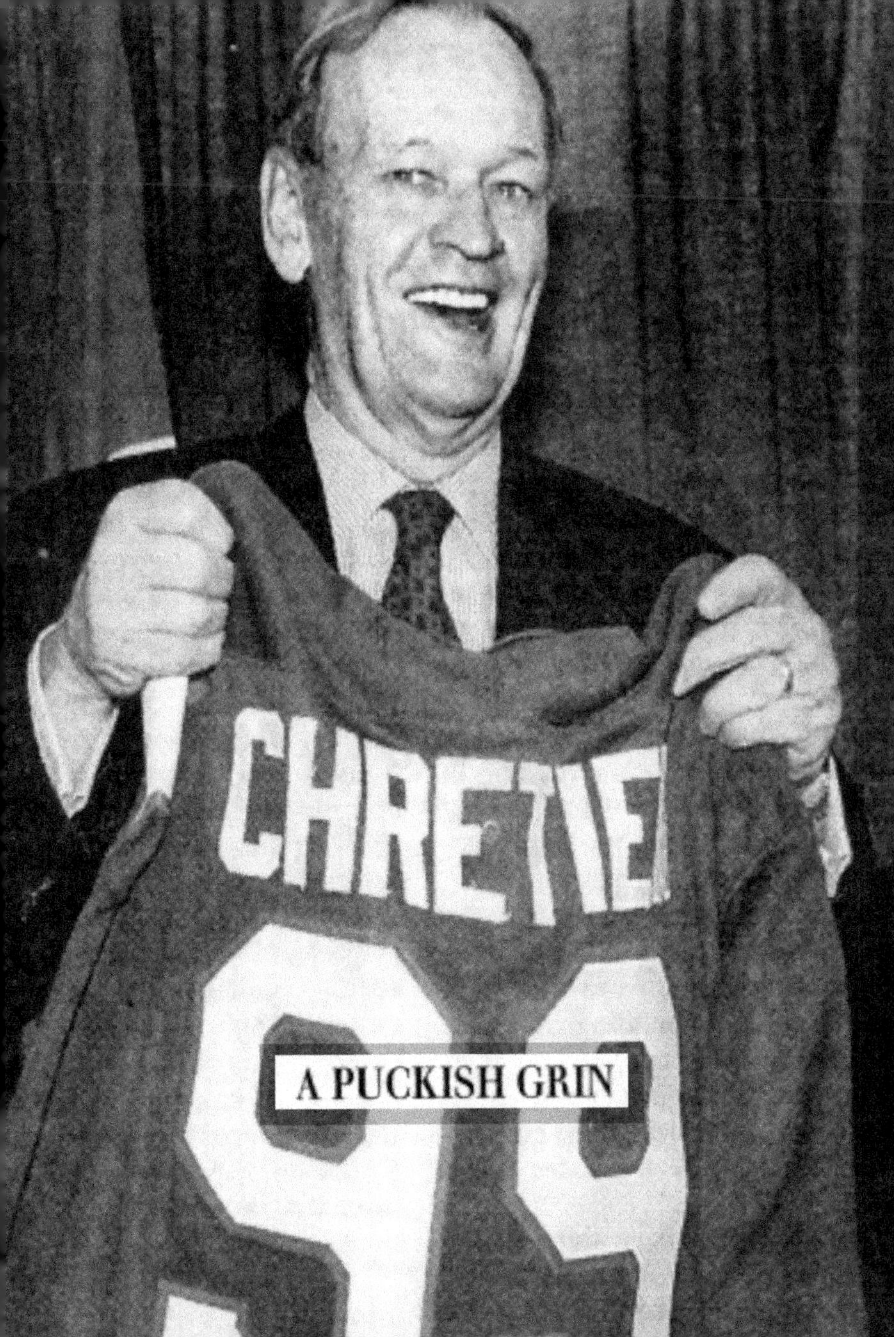

A PUCKISH GRIN

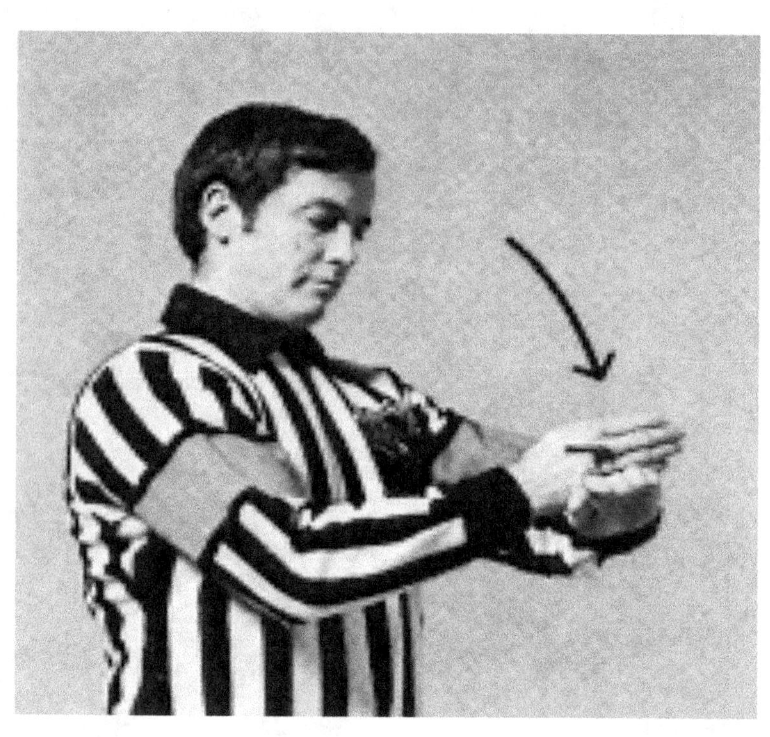

Oligopolists contest bitterly with each other by advertising, by expense-account entertainment, and by industrial espionage, but they do not cut prices. If a price-cutting violation is called by the referee, play stops at once.

The original oligopolists merged into trusts and cartels. Stricter officiating, however, soon either impeded this trend or forced it underground. Anxious to avoid further scrutiny and unfavorable publicity, oligopolists were forced to rely on more circumspect methods of cooperation.

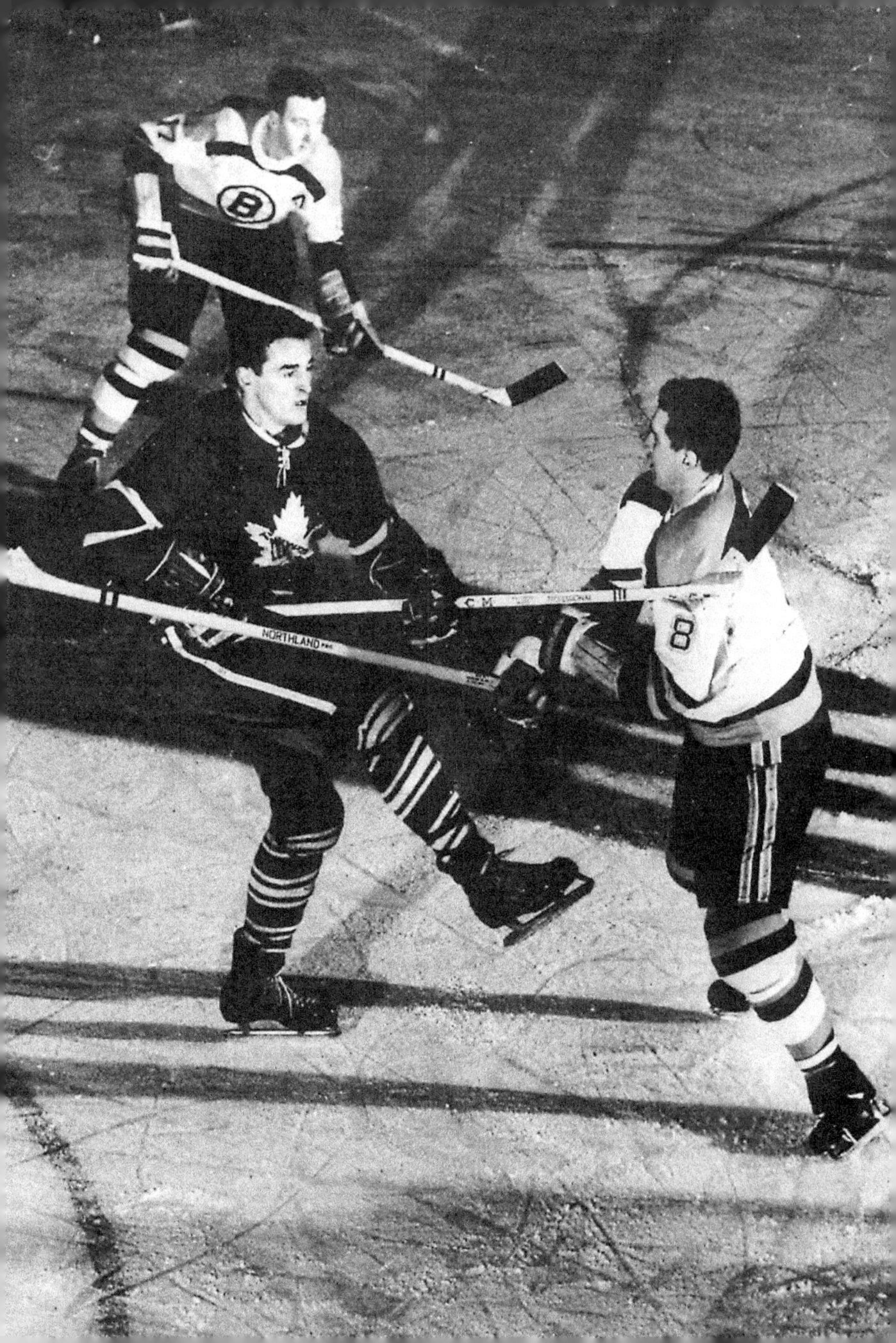
NORTHLAND

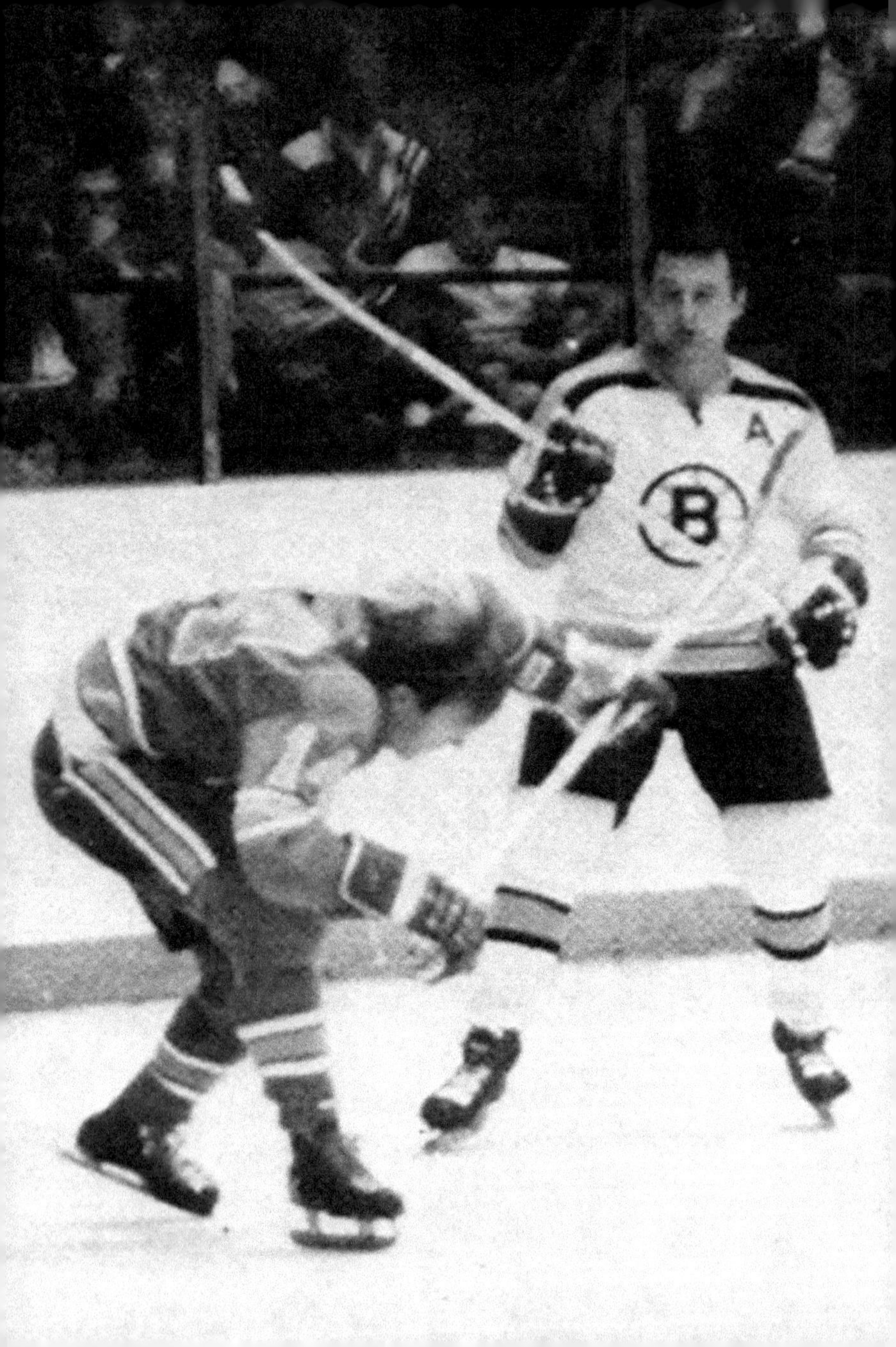

These depended heavily on the observance and enforcement of unwritten behavioral conventions.

"There are rough players and there are dirty players. I'm rough and dirty."

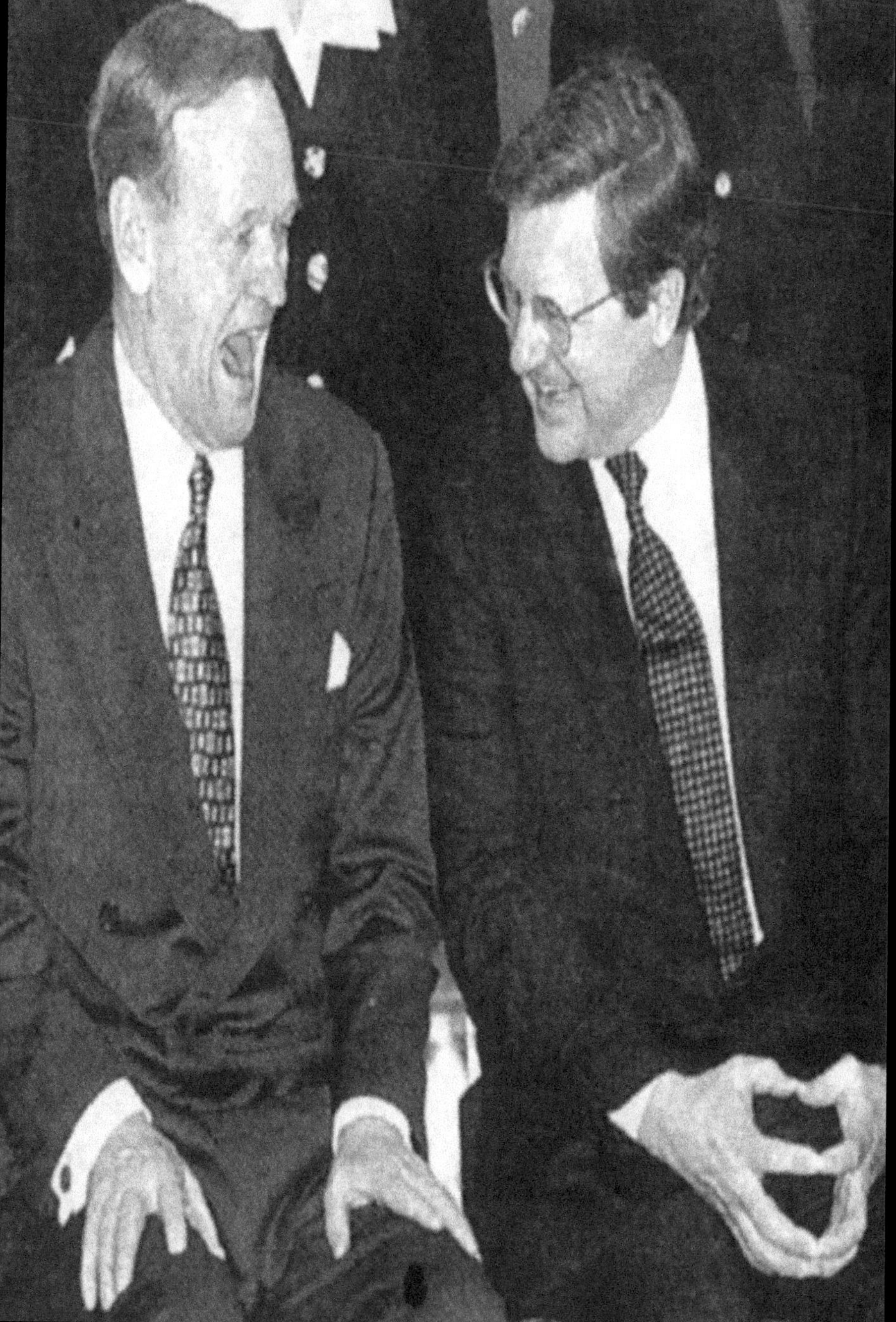

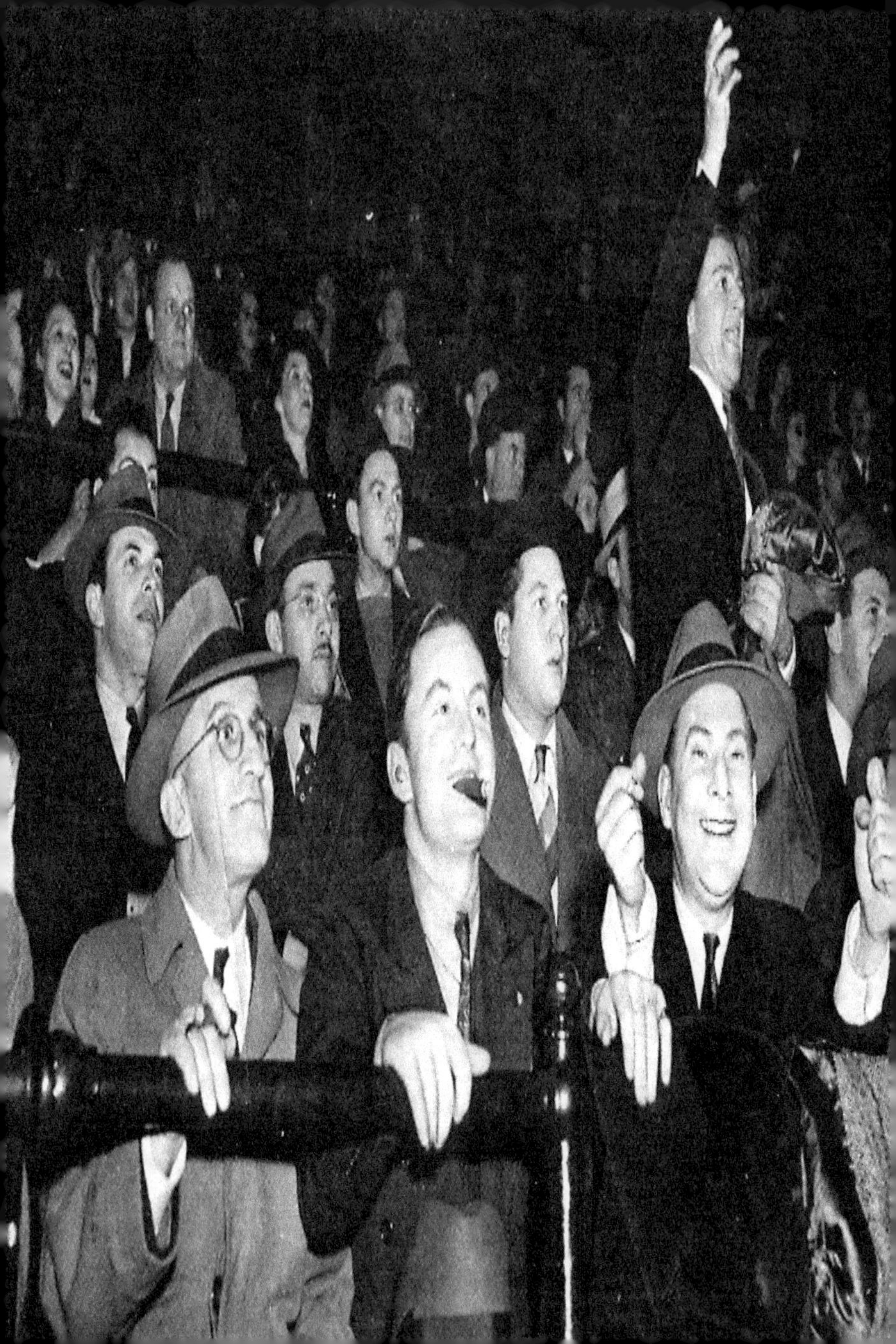

In this clumsy way an oligopolistic industry retains a rough contact with the conditions of production and the desires of its customers.

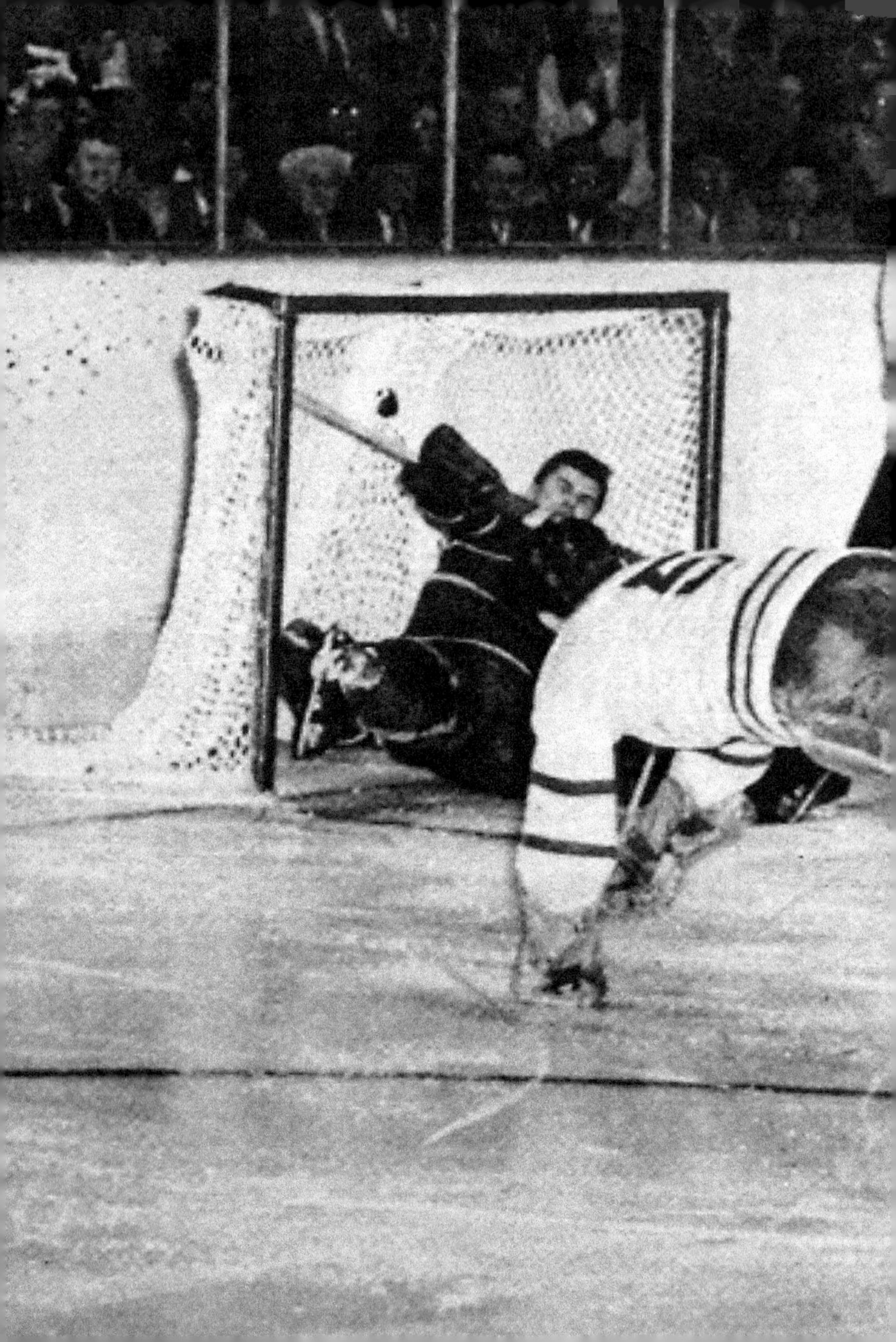

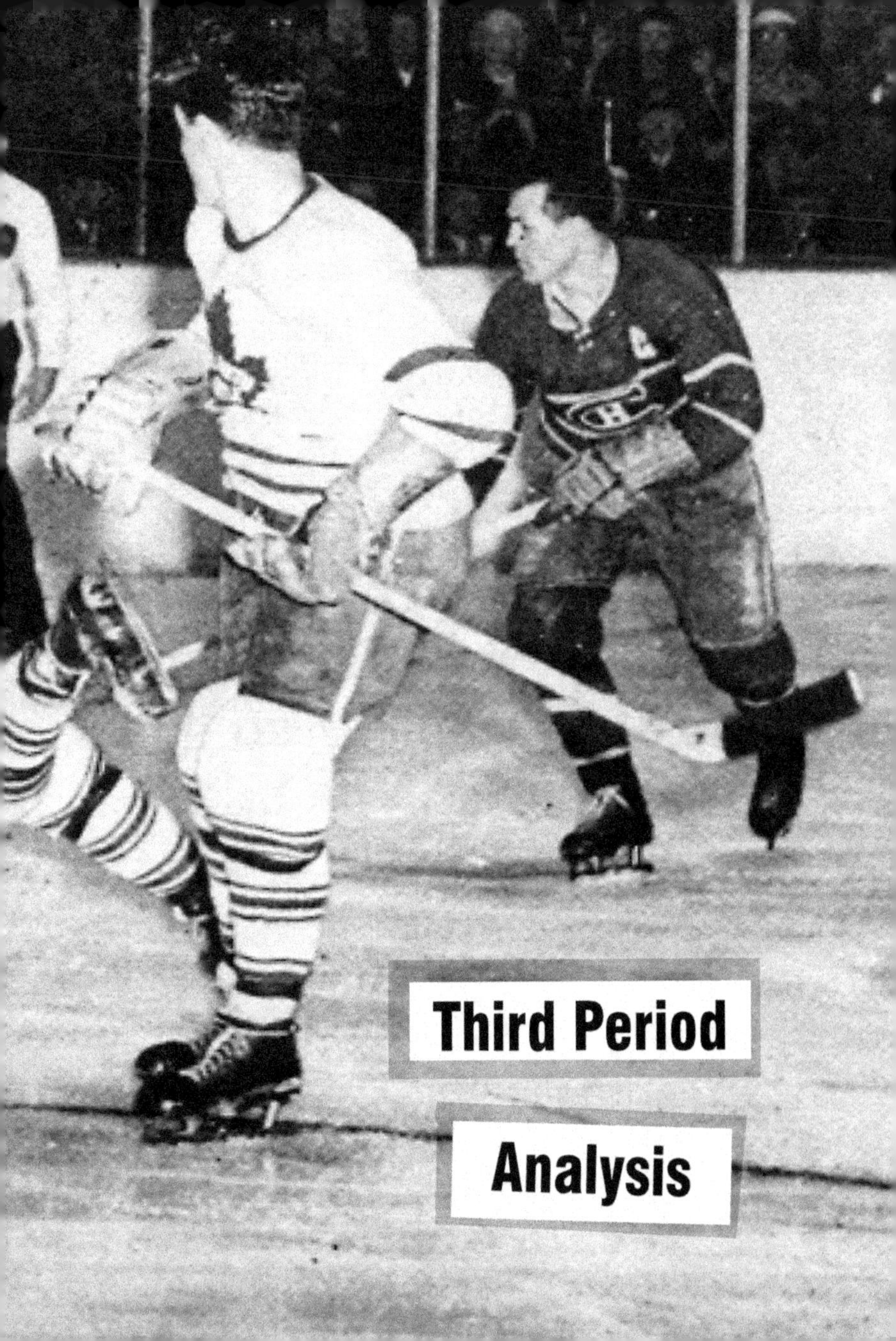
Third Period
Analysis

By now the notion of supporting collusion in infinitely repeated games is quite familiar, so this section will be brief.

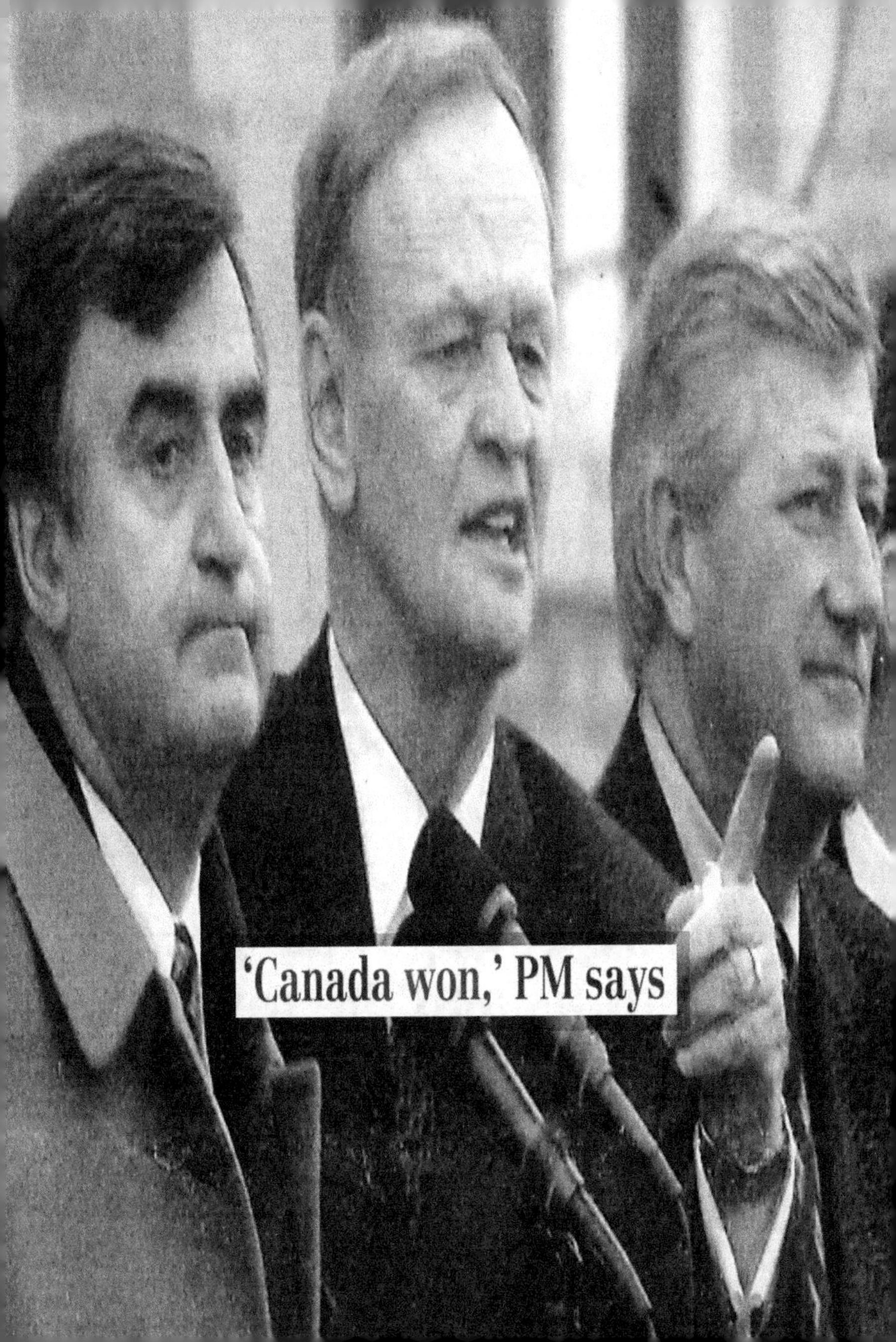
'Canada won,' PM says

In the third period of analysis using the rivalrous consonance technique, we free the consonance factors and permit them to vary endogenously. In doing so we leave the world of the short- and medium-run and struggle for insights into the long-term evolution of mature oligopolies' power structures and the resulting implications for the playoffs.

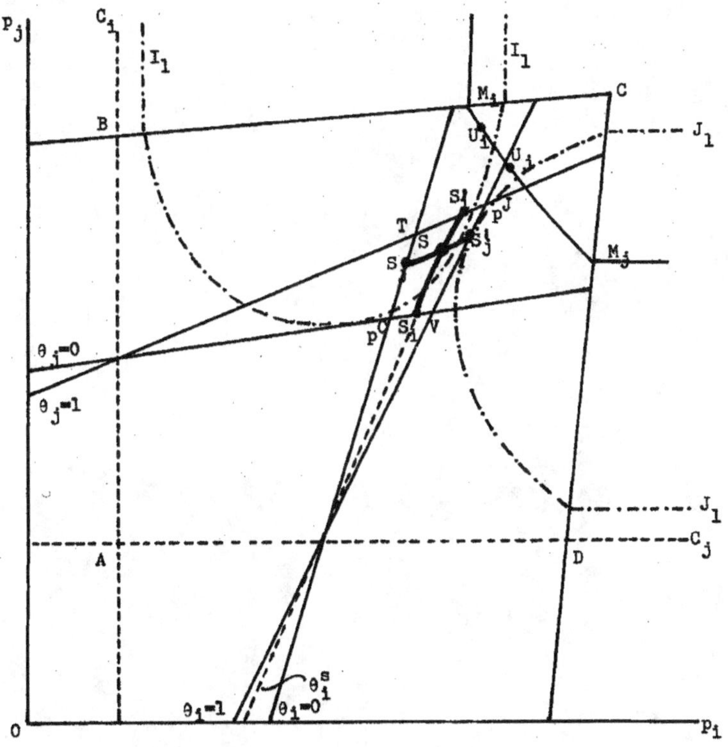

Isoprofit contours and solution regions, with long-run reaction functions.

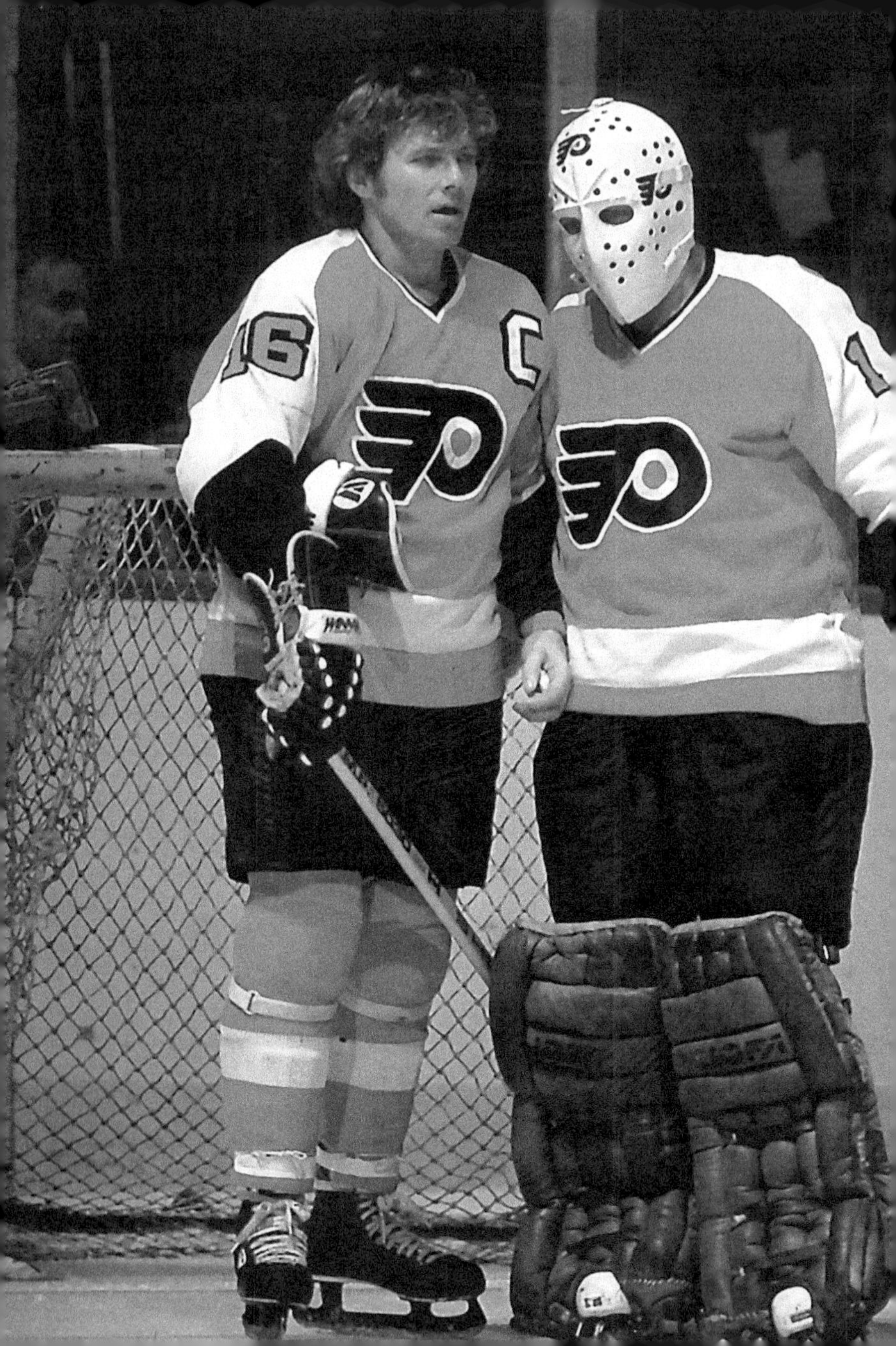
16

From the preceding information, discounted profit functions can be constructed, starting at the second period. If Team 2 does not enter, then Team 1 is a simple monopolist facing no entry threat in the second period, and profit for that period is

$$\pi^{m}_{1}(c_1)=(a-c_1)^2/4b$$

at an output level of

$$q^{m}_{1}(c_1)=(a-c_1)/2b.$$

If Team 2 enters, it is assured that c1 becomes known to it and c2 becomes known to Team 1, and the two teams choose Cournot equilibrium output levels. Thus, their period two profits are: $\pi c1(c1,c2)=(a2c1+c2)2/9b$ and $\pi c2(c1,c2)=(a2c2+c1)2/9b$. Therefore, once the entry decision is made, the rest of the play is determined precisely.

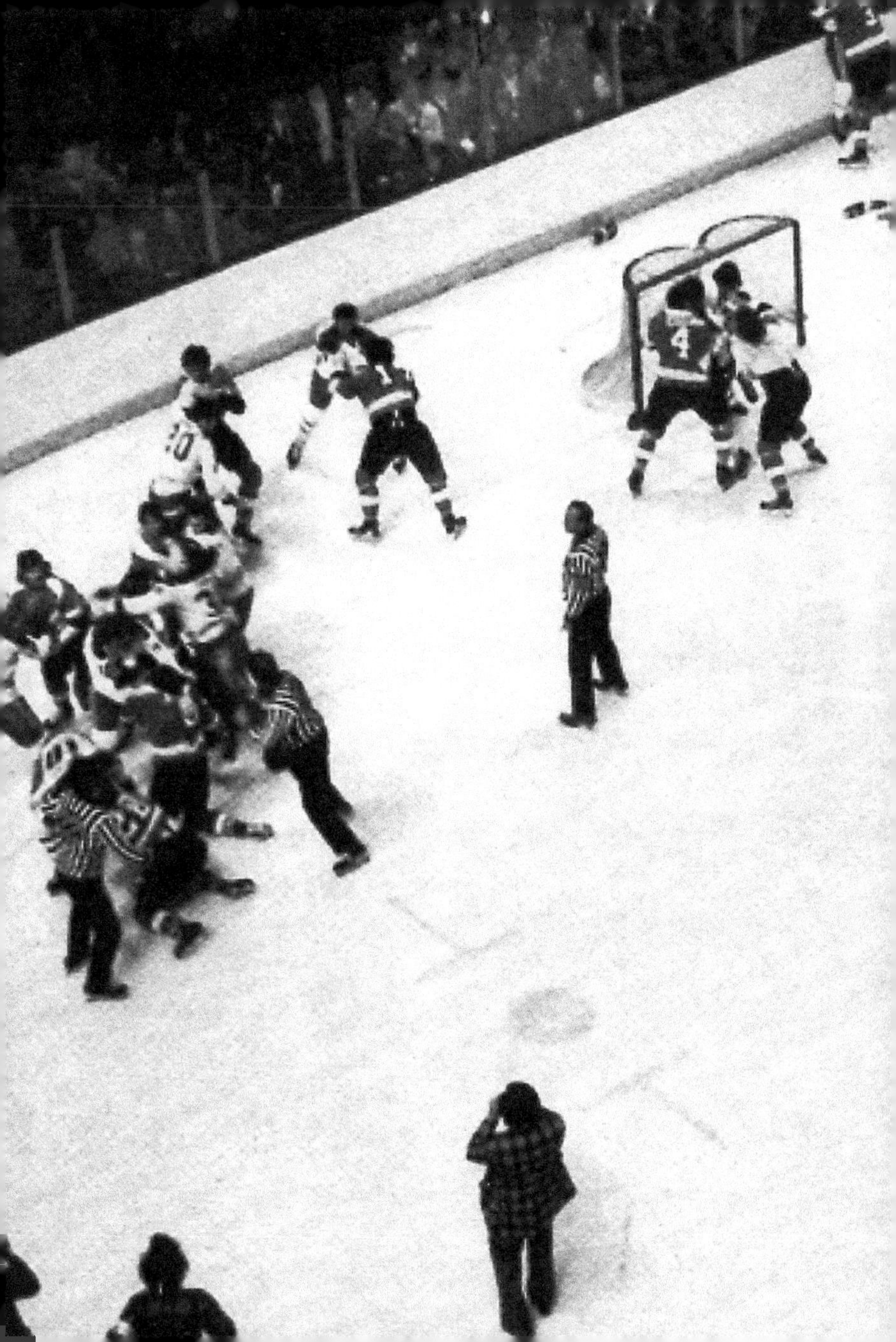

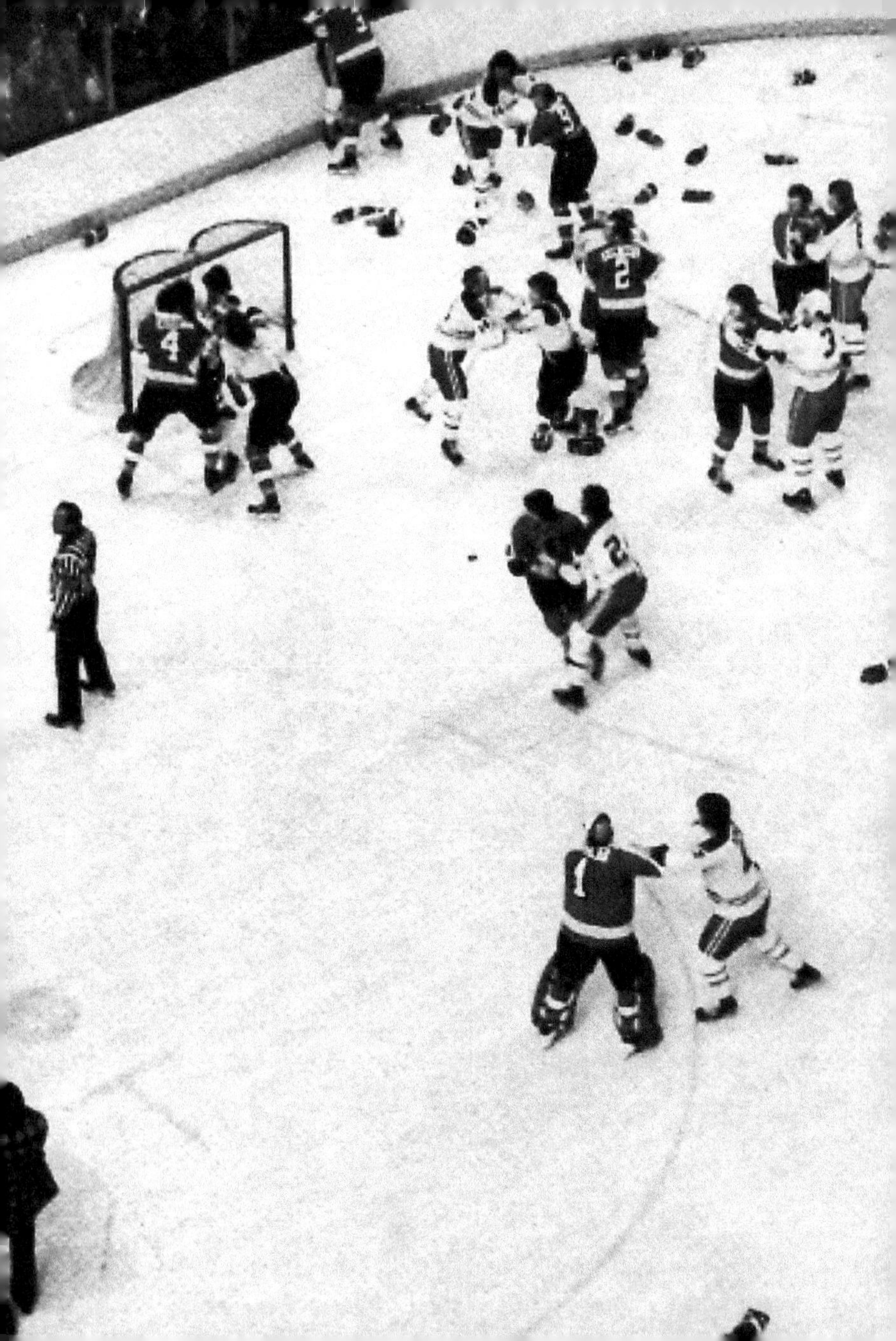

Can anything useful be said about such complicated situations?

Well, sometimes.

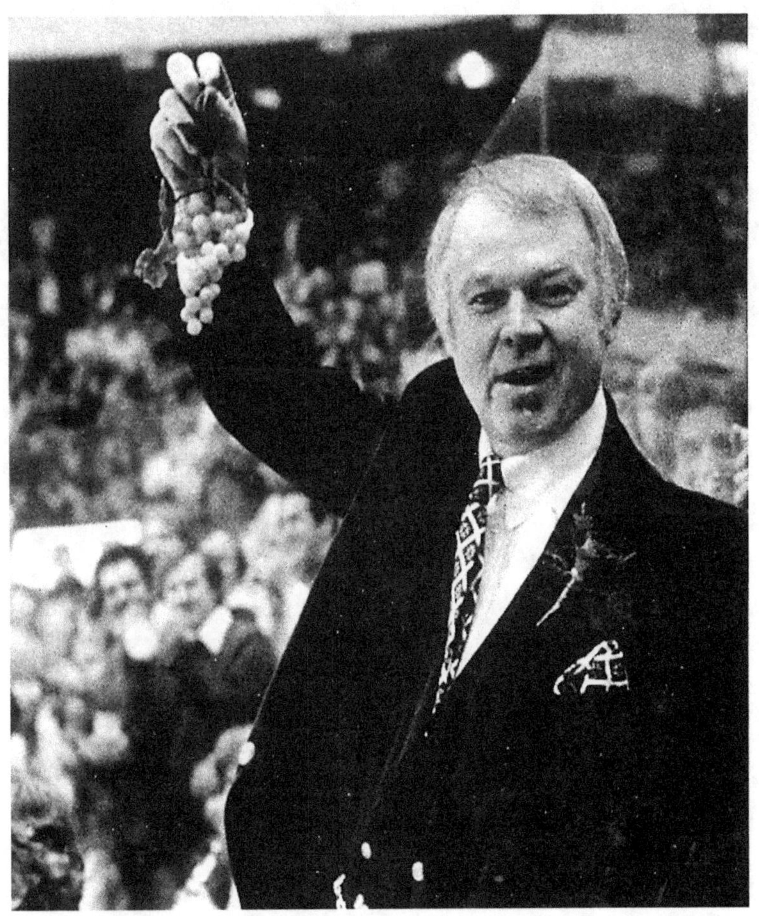

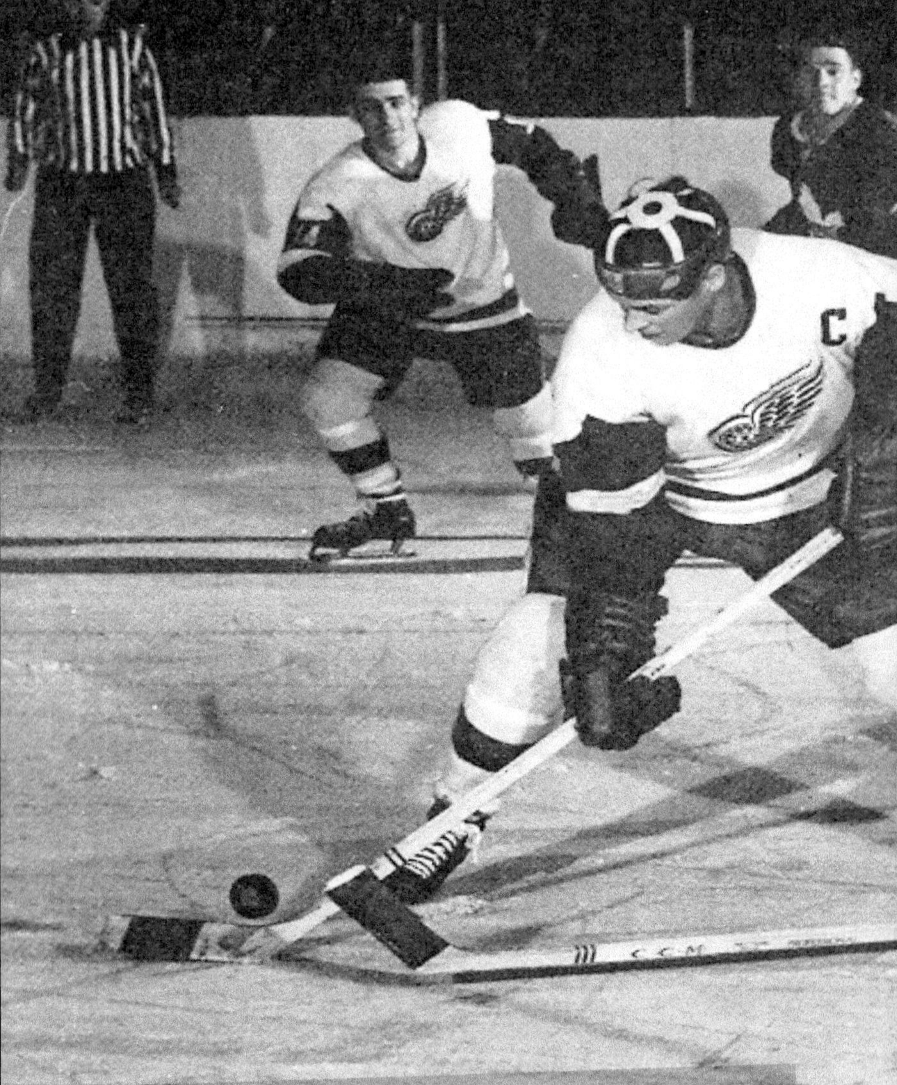

Future Considerations

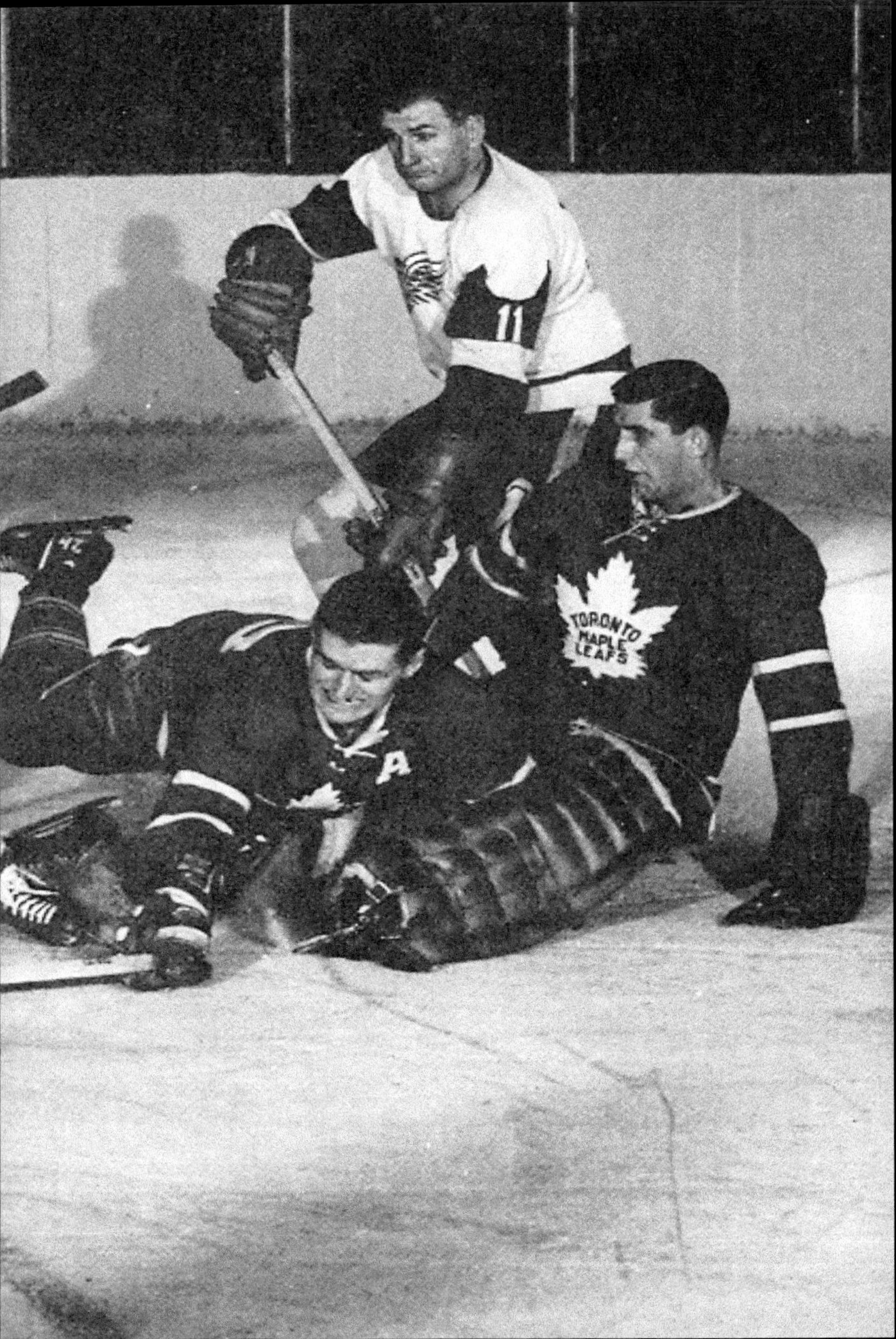
11
TORONTO
MAPLE
LEAFS
A

No effective means for regulating oligopolies have been devised—and it would be unreasonable to expect oligopolists to behave other than as they do; the system of rewards and punishments will tolerate nothing else of them.

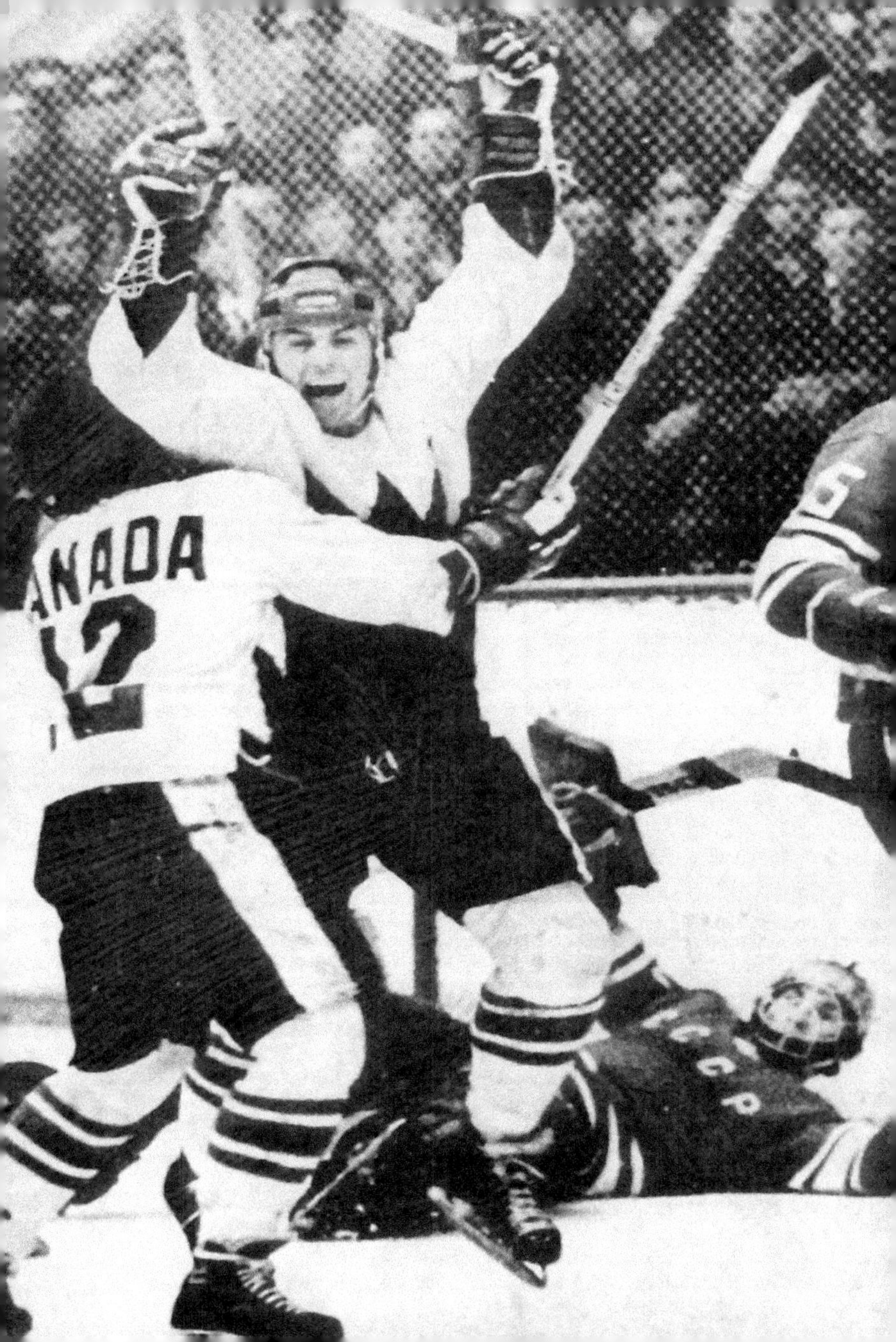

ANADA
12

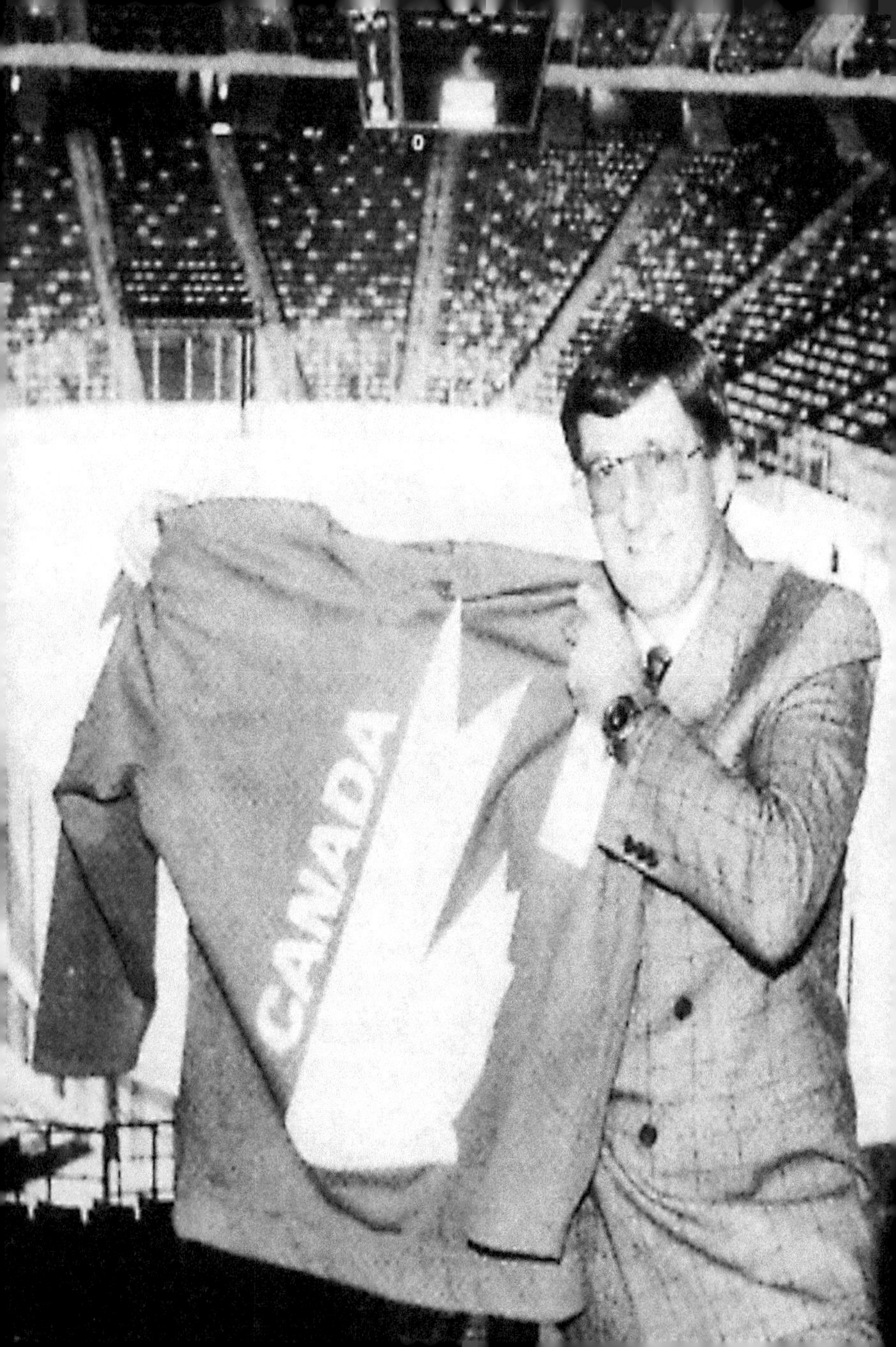
CANADA

Of course, we do not capture in our simple models the rich detail of reality, with all the varying successes, surprises, triumphs, and disasters. We suspect that insightful modelling of such phenomena will only be achieved with simulation enjoying *ex post facto* data.

So long as the oligopolist's thought process is taken to be a compound of the form—"I know that he knows that I know," we may well expect almost anything to emerge from the resulting confusion. Most of the literature has refused to go this far.

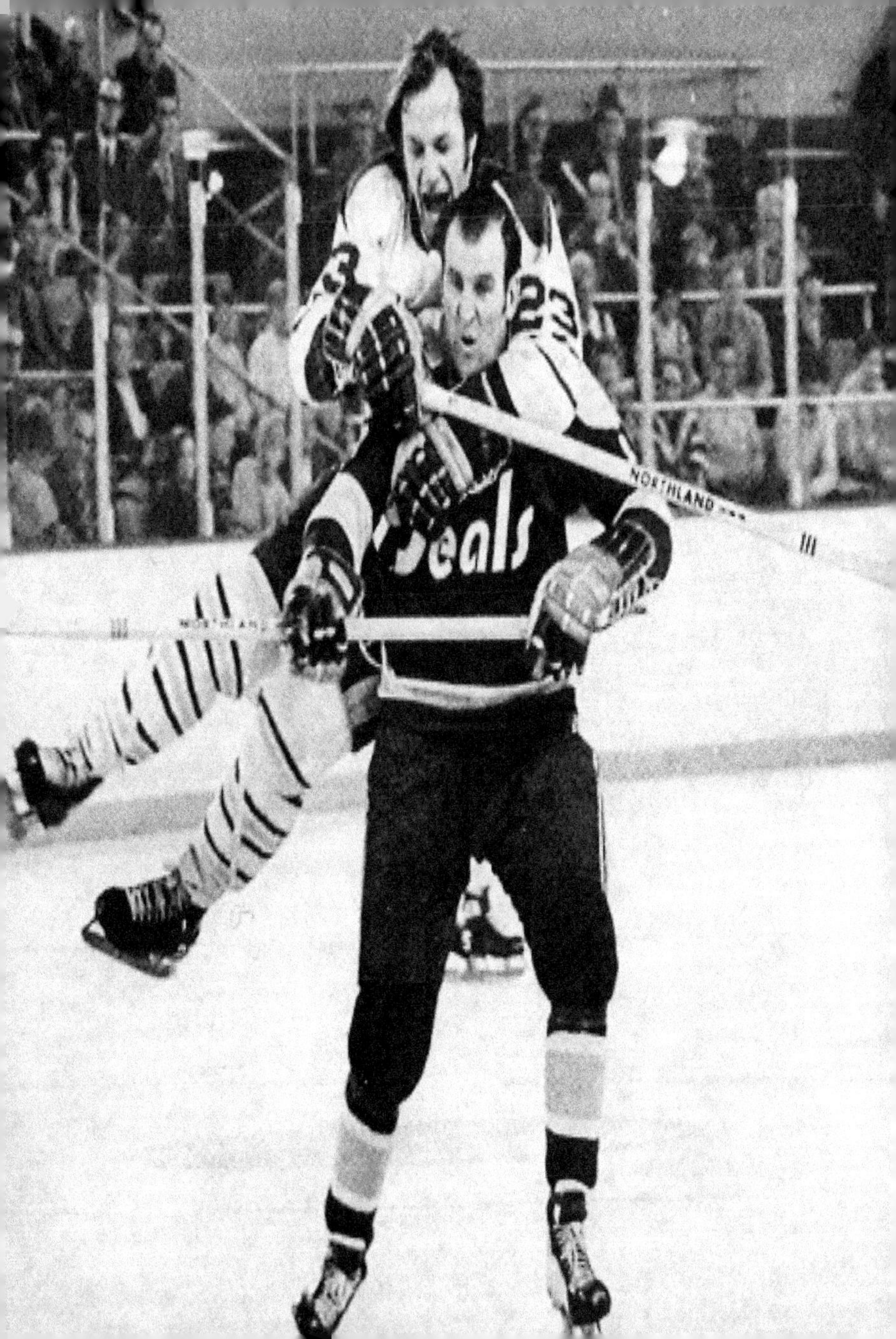
23
Seals
NORTHLAND

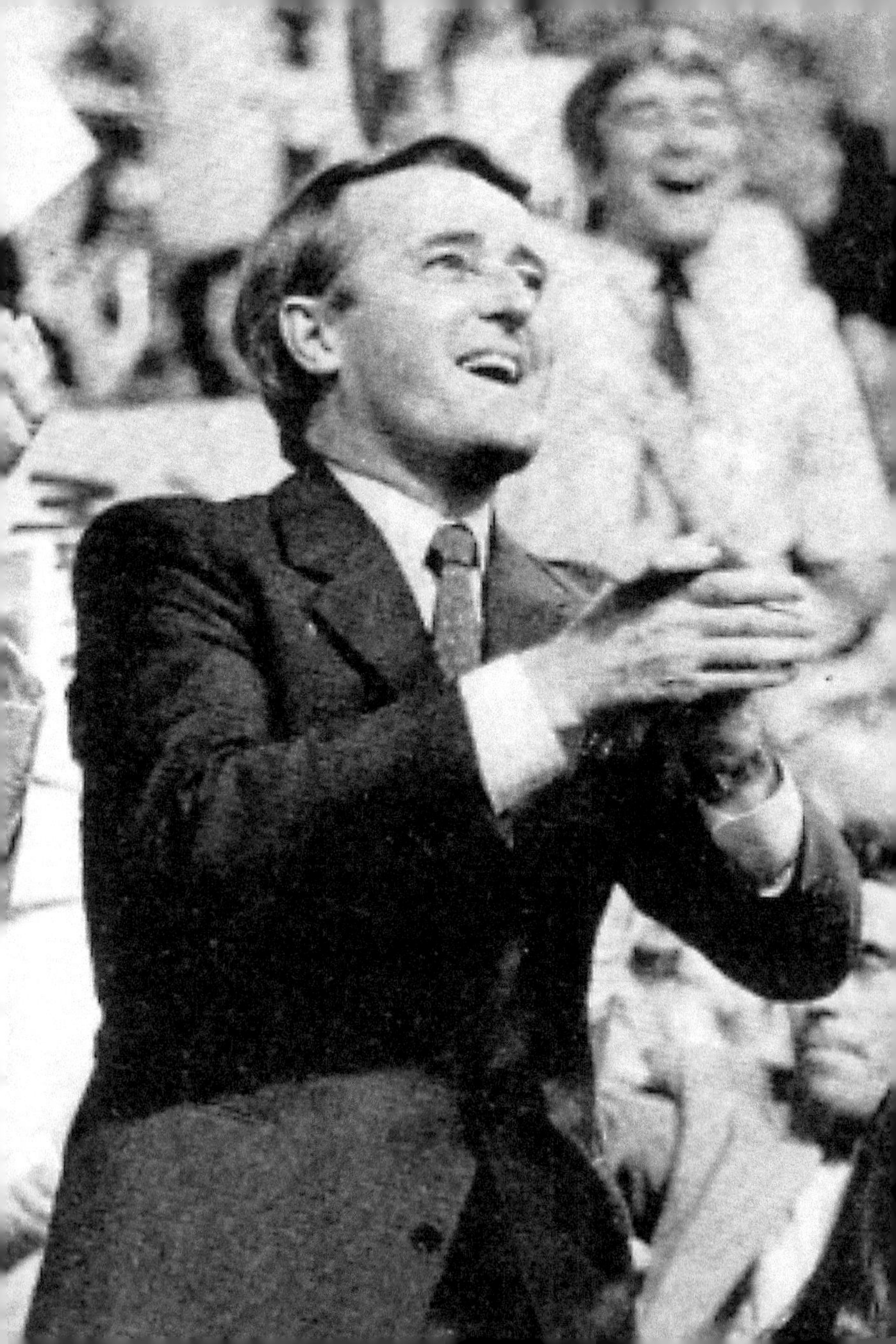

Our ambitions, therefore, are necessarily limited to partial and experimental investigation of the final score, the play of the game, and the three-star selection.

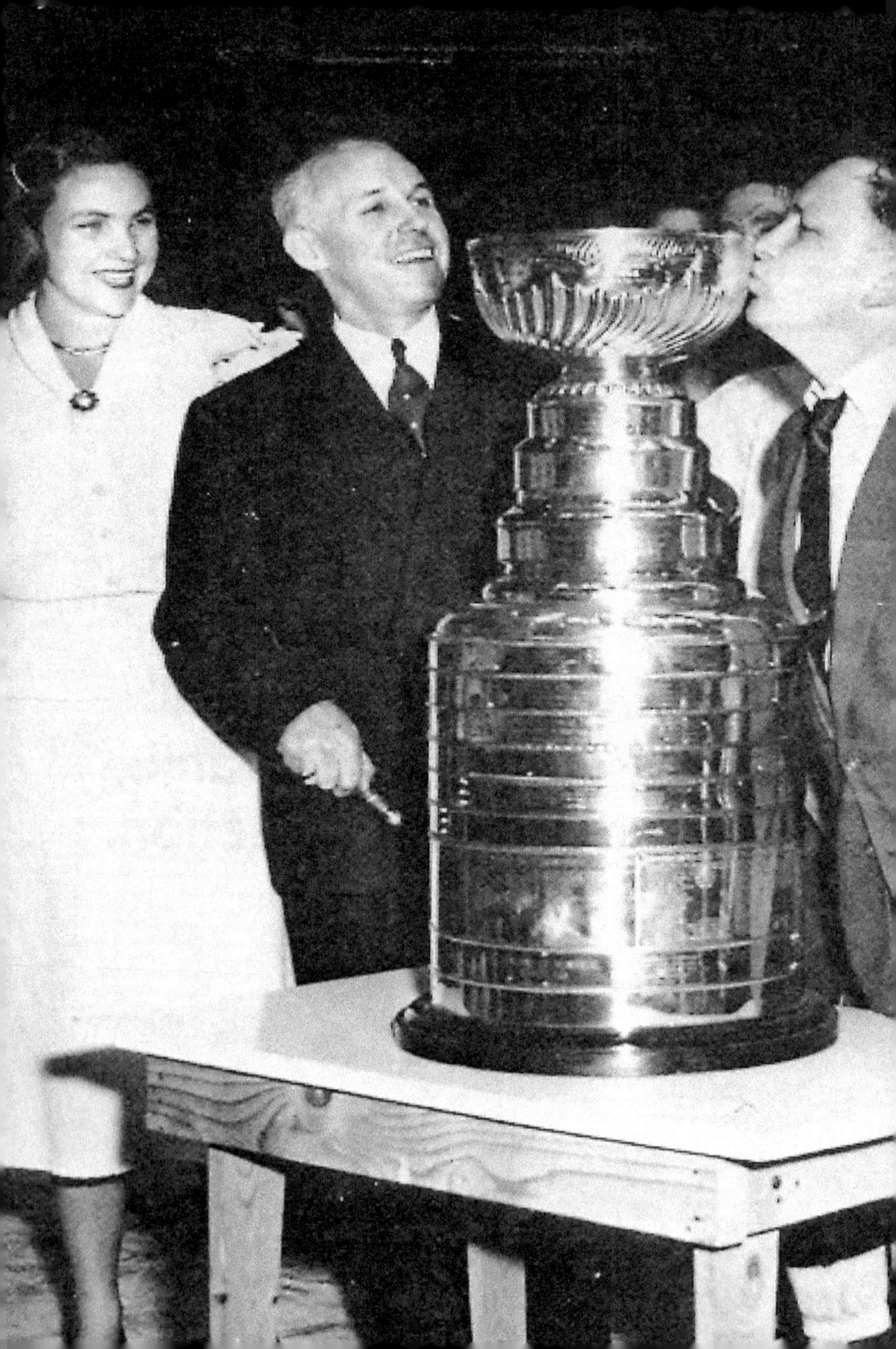

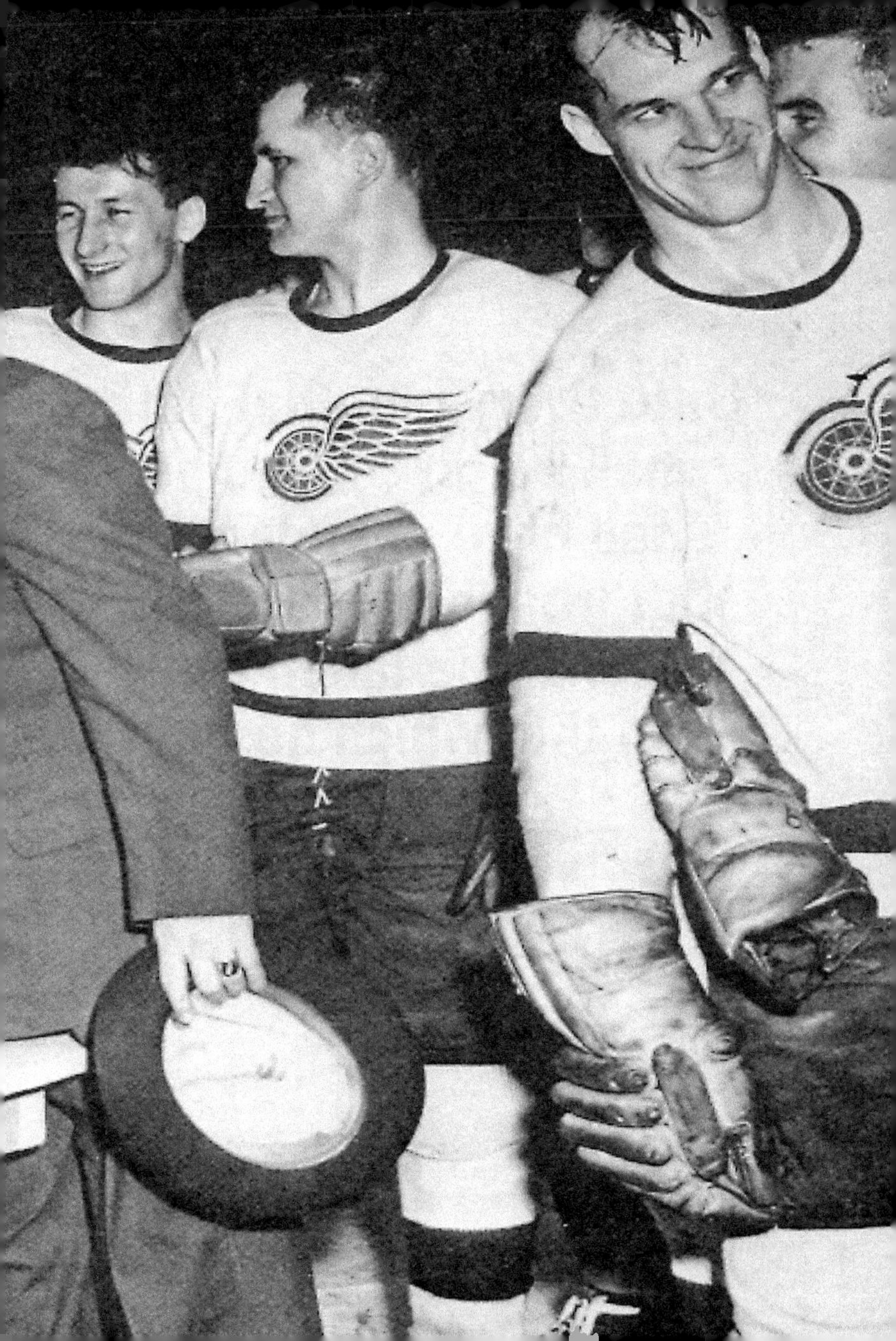

Unto every one that hath shall be given, and he shall have abundance; but from him that hath not shall be taken away even that which he hath.

—Matthew XXV, 29

as quoted in Martin Shubik, Strategy and Market Structure: Competition, Oligopoly, and the Theory of Games

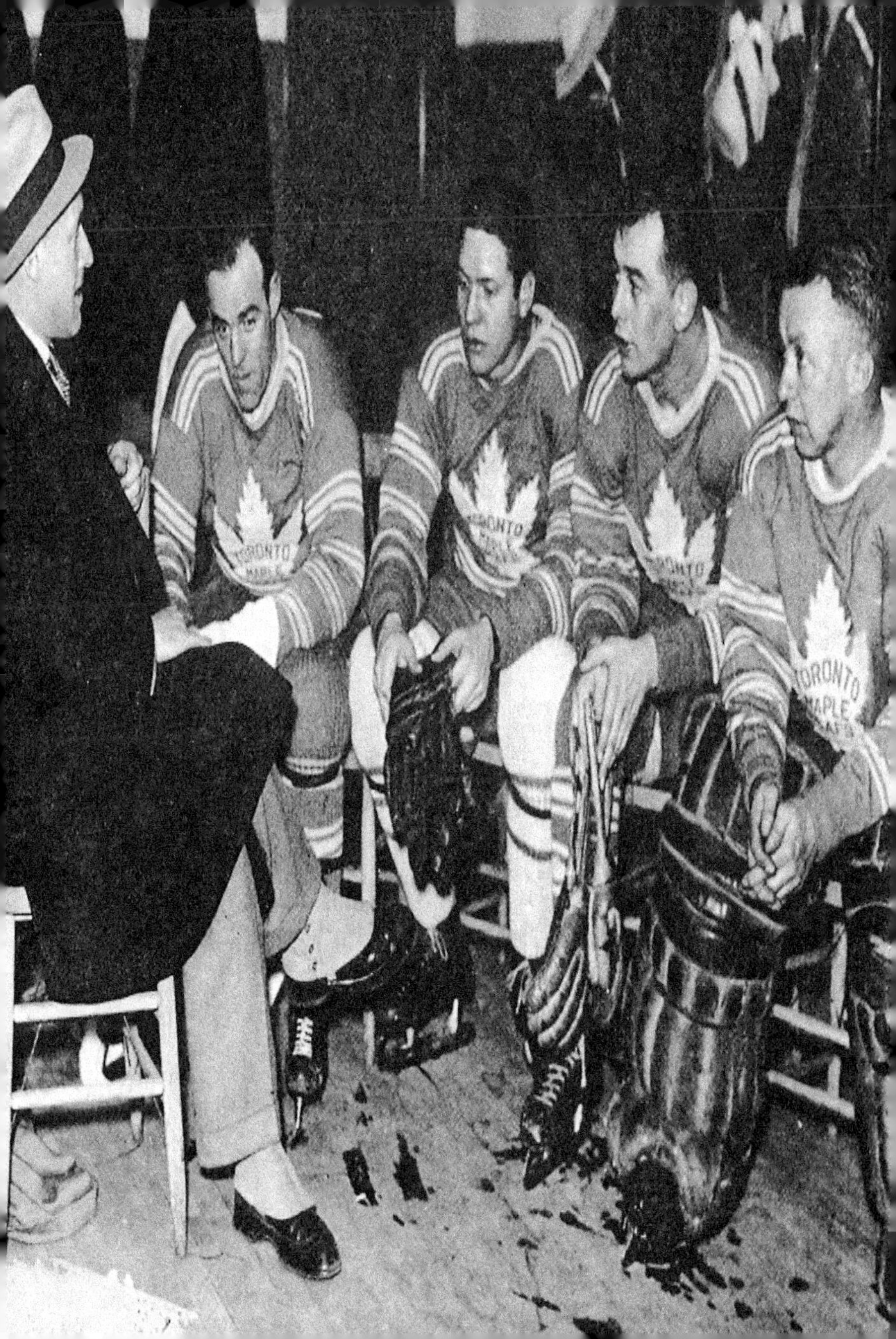
TORONTO
MAPLE

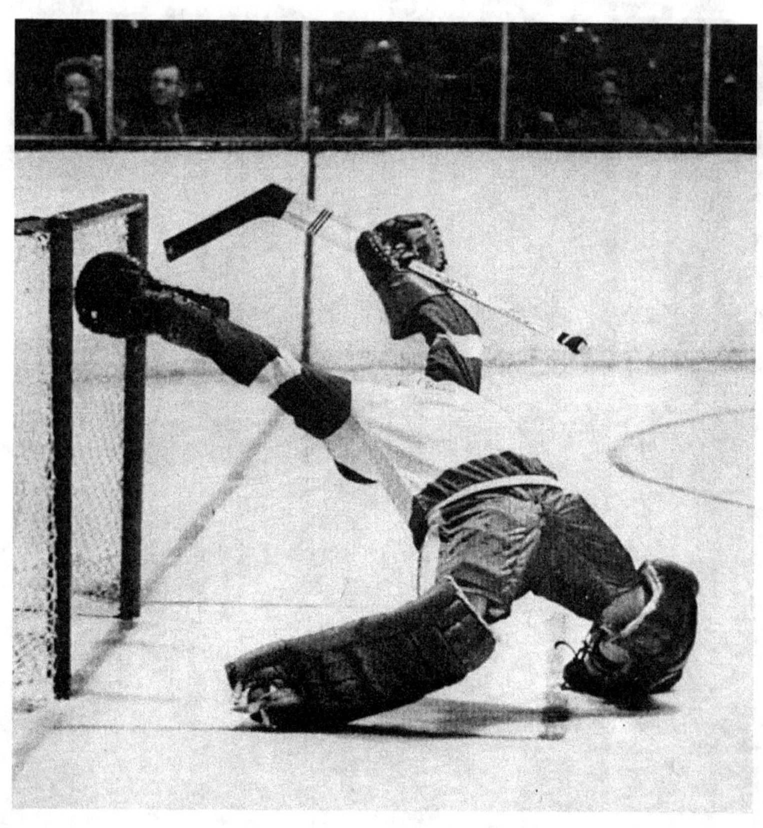

Afterword

This book makes no pretense at being a treatise. No attempt has been made to offer a well-rounded discussion of any of its subjects. The reader will doubtless note many serious omissions and cases wherein important elements are inadequately stressed. These he will have to supply for himself or apply from elsewhere in the literature ...

In almost every case I included items only where I felt I had something, however minor, to contribute in novelty of analysis or exposition. I hope it is not too much of an abuse of the reader to ask him to put up with the unbalanced treatments which result.

William J. Baumol, Business Behavior and Growth

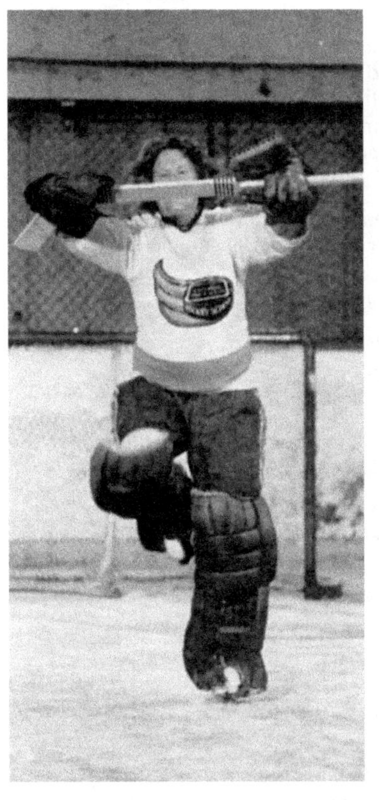

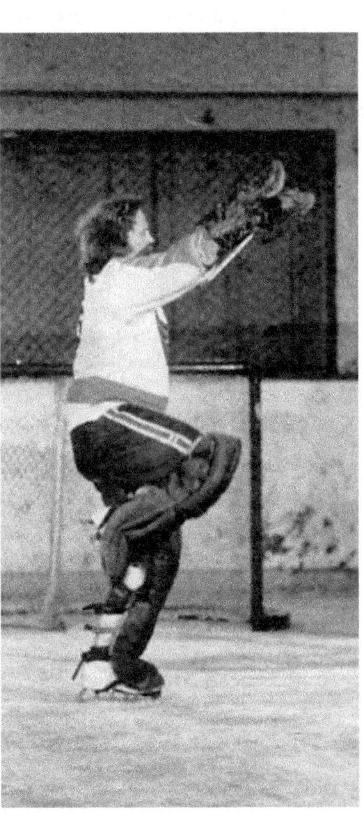

Sources

The text of this book consists of quotes culled verbatim from a number of economic textbooks, various books and articles on hockey, and from daily newspapers. These, as well as the photos, are combined, juxtaposed and ordered by the author in a completely subjective manner. In some cases, texts from two different sources are combined on the same page, or in the same sentence. The following are the sources of the texts and photos used in this project:

"The Game of Ice Hockey." *The Book of Knowledge Children's Encyclopedia.* Toronto: Grolier Society of Canada Ltd., 1955, pp. 6520-22.

Baumol, William J. *Business Behavior, Value and Growth.* New York: The Macmillan Company, 1959.

Cherry, Don, with Stan Fischler. *Grapes: A Vintage View of Hockey.* Scarborough, Ontario: Prentice-Hall Canada, Inc., 1982.

Diamond, Dan, and Charles Wilkins. *Hockey: The Illustrated History.* Toronto: Doubleday, 1989.

Diamond, Dan, ed. *The Official National Hockey League Stanley Cup Centennial Book.* Toronto: McClelland & Stewart, 1991.

Dorfman, Robert. *Prices and Markets.* Englewood Cliffs, New Jersey: Prentice-Hall, Inc., 1967.

Dreayer, Barry. *Teach Me Sports: Hockey.* Los Angeles: General Publishing Group, 1995.

Friedman, James. *Oligopoly Theory.* Cambridge: Cambridge University Press, 1983.

Globe and Mail, Toronto, various dates, 1996.

Green, Ted, with Al Hirshberg. *High Stick.* New York: Dodd, Mead and Company, 1971.

Houston, William, and David Shoalts. *Eagleson: The Fall of a Hockey Czar.* Toronto: McGraw-Hill Ryerson, 1993.

Howe, Gordie. "Hockey." *World Book Encyclopedia Annual Supplement.* Chicago: World Book, 1961, pp. 552-8.

Kuenne, Robert E. *Rivalrous Consonance: A Theory of General Oligopolistic Equilibrium.* Amsterdam: Elsevier Science Publishers, 1986.

McFarlane, Brian. *One Hundred Years of Hockey.* Toronto: Deneau, 1989.

McDonald, Marci. *Yankee Doodle Dandy: Brian Mulroney and the American Agenda.* Toronto: Stoddart, 1995.

Meeker, Howie. *More Hockey Basics.* Scarborough, Ontario: Prentice-Hall of Canada, 1975.

Ross, Thomas. *Cartel Stability and Product Differentiation.* Ottawa: Department of Economics, Carleton University, 1990.

Sawatsky, John. *Mulroney: The Politics of Ambition.* Toronto: Macfarlane Walter & Ross, 1991.

Shubik, Martin. *Strategy and Market Structure: Competition, Oligopoly, and the Theory of Games.* New York: John Wiley & Sons, 1959.

Stein, Gil. *Power Plays: An Inside Look at the Big Business of the National Hockey League.* Secaucus, N.J.: Carol Publishing Group, 1997.

Stenlund, Vern. *Hockey Drills for Puck Control.* Windsor, Ontario: Human Kinetics, 1996.

Toronto Star, Feb. 26, 1996.

Winnipeg Free Press. Feb. 5, 1999.

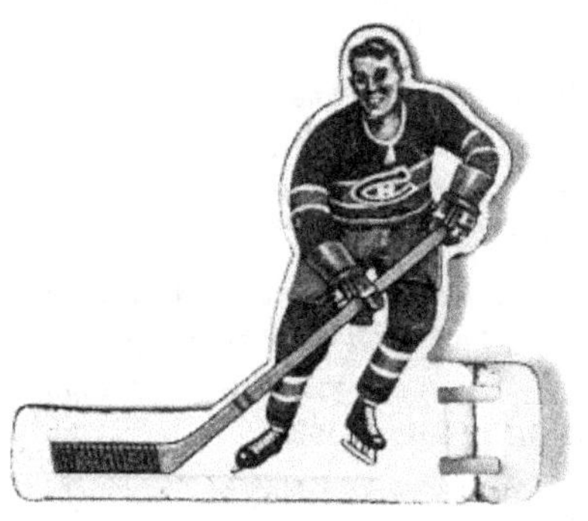

Treyf?

treyf, adj. [Yiddish]—not kosher, unclean.

Treyf—unusual books of an indeterminate type, sort of story-picture remix books for people who can't stomach any more schmaltzy *Chicken Soup for the Soul.* Treyf is cooked up using texts and images collected from various sources, usually obsessively related to one or more themes, and then recombined through a process of highly subjective editing, ordering and juxtaposition.

"Strange and clever." — Globe & Mail

"Funny, but deep." — Umbrella

"Is this a new form of discourse in step with its multivalent, chaotic times, or just an excuse for intellectual laziness? Only the author knows for sure." — Canadian Architect

www.treyf.com
keep refrigerated

www.ingramcontent.com/pod-product-compliance
Lightning Source LLC
Chambersburg PA
CBHW051005050726
47592CB00007B/2718

9780981286976